THE DRAGONS REBELLIOUS SACRIFICE

THE LAST DRAGONS BOOK 4

INES JOHNSON

THOSE JOHNSON GIRLS

Copyright © 2021, Ines Johnson. All rights reserved.
This novel is a work of fiction. All characters, places, and incidents described in this publication are used fictitiously, or are entirely fictional. No part of this publication may be reproduced or transmitted, in any form or by any means, except by an authorized retailer, or with written permission of the author.

Edited by Alyssa Breck
Cover design by Jacqueline Sweet Designs

CHAPTER ONE

For a dragon who had come into the world with two siblings, Ilia did not enjoy his solitude. He sat at the end of the bar. The seat to his right empty. The seat to his left had clattered down onto the floor sometime ago when its last occupant had vacated it. True, the troll who had been sitting there when Ilia had arrived had taken one look at Ilia's sharp-toothed snarl and fled. But that was beside the point.

Ilia did not want to be alone.

"Is this seat taken?" purred a high-pitched voice.

The enticing scent coming off the pink-skinned fairy tugged at Ilia's nostrils. He hunched over his drink instead, breathing in and letting the fiery alcohol burn the perfume from his nose hairs.

"You want some company tonight, Ilia?" The fairy moved the standing barstool out of the way and aimed her pert ass for Ilia's lap. "Clove and I would be happy to keep you up all night and into the morning."

Clove, the mint green fairy, came up behind Ilia. Her earthy scent clashed with the saccharine scent of the lavender of Honeysuckle. Their hands wrapped around Ilia's biceps like vines twining around a tree's trunk.

A few weeks ago, Ilia would've welcomed the distraction of two fairies' attentions. Hell, he'd have walked naked through a whole garden of the beauties and fertilized them all. Now, the feel of these two made his skin crawl. The smell of them made his stomach turn. Because neither of them was *her*.

"Not tonight," Ilia said, shrugging them off gently. Or at least as gently as he could.

He was a large dragon, known more for his strength and prowess than his tender touch. Most fairies, with their flexible limbs, liked it a little rough.

"Why not?" said Clove. "You think we're not enough for you? You can have us both at the same-"

"I said no."

Fire huffed out of Ilia's nose. The two fairies

backed off immediately, knocking the chair to his right over to join the left in their haste to move away from him.

Ilia knew he should apologize. It was very bad manners to scare off defenseless females. It was not chivalrous behavior. Nothing like his idol Arnold "The Terminator" Schwarzenegger, who would've dipped his sunshades and told them he'd be back.

But he didn't go back for the two fairies. He didn't want to be their hero. He wanted to be *her* hero. But she wasn't here.

Ilia picked up his drink and threw the contents down his throat. The fiery liquid burned going down. Literally. There were flames coming out of the mug. But for a fire-breathing dragon, it was just a tickle as it slid down and into his belly. What really bothered Ilia was being alone.

In a world where dragons were born in pairs, Ilia had been the third in a set of triplets. He'd been born the runt of the litter. He'd come out last; too small, too weak to live. And yet, he had survived.

"What's wrong? Not hot enough for you, big guy?"

Ilia took a deep breath, ready to breathe fire at the new interruption into his pity party. When he lifted his head, there was no eager fairy standing to his right or his left. This fairy was standing behind the bar, looking at him with a quizzical brow raised.

"I'm not in the mood, Mari," Ilia said, throwing a glance over his shoulder at the still retreating fairies.

"I didn't mean the pansy twins. I meant the drink." Mari pointed at the empty mug on the bar.

Ilia stared into the bottom of the glass. It was vacant of any drops of liquid. And also of any licks of flame.

Mari swiped the mug from him and turned to refill it. Amber liquid poured into the mug. The color of a bright flame waiting to be ignited.

"What's gotten into you?" she asked. "You're usually in the back corner of the bar with a couple of fairies wrapped around your waist."

"That's not me. Not anymore."

"That's all dragons," Mari snorted. "And lions, and bears, and wolves. All you beasts think fairies are your own personal harem."

With a flick of her delicate wrists, Mari struck a match and lit the drink. Flames ignited, flowing over the rim of the cup. She shoved the mug to him and stepped back as the fire lifted.

Mari's lips curled in a grimace of distaste. Fairies liked warmth, but not fire, which could singe their cellulose skin. Mari's skin was completely covered by a formless sack of brown that did nothing for her indigo complexion. It didn't matter. She was still breathtaking. Fairies were beautiful no matter if they smiled or frowned, were naked or covered in mud. Just like the flowers they evolved from, it was in their nature to draw the eye of any man or beast that came near.

Ilia had never come near Mari. Not in that way. She was his friend. Heroes didn't fuck their friends. They practiced on nameless wenches while they waited for their true love to call out for them to rescue her.

Ilia closed his eyes and listened closely. All he heard was the chatter of fairies, trolls, and a couple of beasts. *She* wasn't here in this bar. *She* wasn't here in this realm.

"You look like death," Mari was saying. "And your nails are dirty. Is that blood?"

Ilia nodded as he lifted the mug and took a sniff. A flame scorched the tip of his nose. "I killed my father earlier."

The sound of his father's bones crunching under the weight of Ilia's claws sent a shiver of satisfaction down his spine. The sound of bones cracking and breaking was all too familiar to Ilia's ears. After all, his father had broken his bones repeatedly when he was just a fledgling. Left him broken, battered, and bruised. Left him for dead.

But Ilia, the stubborn dragon that he was, kept healing. He kept breathing. He kept living.

Mari's sky blue gaze met his. Ilia knew that wasn't fear in her eyes, at least not fear of him. She'd seen him during those times as a defenseless whelp. She and his brothers had tended to Ilia... the few times he'd let them.

"So the old dragon is truly dead?" Mari asked.

In answer, Ilia took a swig of his drink. Mari had increased the flame. It scalded his throat and took him a minute before he could speak.

Mari leaned over the bar and bent her head close to Ilia's. Her scent was more spicy than sweet. "Good riddance."

Fairies didn't have blood lust. Likely because they didn't have any blood. They were all sap inside.

Not Mari.

There was a touch of ice in her. Too bad she wasn't his mate. It would've made Ilia's life simpler. But fae and dragons were not compatible. They could never procreate. Since Mari couldn't give him any whelps of his own, his dragon would always reject her. The beast wanted a human female. But those were rare creatures in this part of the world.

In the last ten years, only three human women had come from beyond the Veil. Poppy had come to this side of the Veil a few weeks ago. But Ilia's brother Beryl had claimed her after a battle where Beryl had fought dirty. Ilia was still pissed at the low blow his brother had dealt him in that clash.

A few weeks before that, Chryssie had been placed in his older brother Corun's lap. Corun had said he didn't want the fiery redhead. But the moment Ilia declared his intentions, Corun had taken back his word and snatched Chryssie up.

It was bad form in heroic combat, and Ilia had told his brother so. But Corun didn't care. He was too busy wrapping Chryssie's legs around his waist.

Years before that, Cardi had been dropped on their doorstep. She'd been an unripe kid back then. Kimber, their eldest brother, had won her after battling their father. But Kimber hadn't touched Cardi all these years. Until their father came back to call dibs on the now-grown woman.

"I was the hero today," Ilia said. "I vanquished the villain. But I still didn't manage to get the damsel. How is that fair?"

"You mean when you saved Cardi from your father?" asked Mari. "Wait? You're in love with Cardi?"

"No, I'm not in love with Cardi. She's practically my sister, like you. But I did save her. And do I get any thanks?"

"I'm guessing no."

Mari guessed correctly. Ilia had saved Cardi from a fate worse than death. And what thanks did he get from her? A door slammed in his face.

"She didn't even want a sleepover. She's in bed with Kimber now. And, trust me, they're not sleeping."

"There's plenty of females who would love a sleepover with you. And none of them would want to sleep."

"It's not the same with a fairy. No offense."

Mari held up her hands, showing that she was neither open to offense or sleeping with Ilia.

"She should be here by now." Ilia turned, looking at the closed door of the bar.

"Who?"

"My mate. What if she's not here because she's in danger? I should go to her. The Terminator went after Sarah Connor. He broke the time barrier to do it."

"Didn't the Terminator go through time to kill Sarah Connor?"

Ilia thrummed his fingers on the empty mug. It

was still warm. "What if Reese was there now, telling her lies about me?"

"You do know that Kyle Reese was the hero of that film and not the Terminator."

Ilia stood, shoving the barstool to the ground. It landed with a thud next to the other two. "I need to go find her."

"You can't go beyond the Veil, Ilia."

"The Valkyries opened the Veil. So there's nothing stopping me. I could go and find her for myself. How hard can it be?"

"You know there are millions of humans out there."

"There's also the Book of Yellow Pages. That's how Arnold found Sarah Connor. I swear, did you even watch the movie?"

"Did you?"

Of course, he did. It was his favorite film of all time. With *T2* being a close second when Arnold comes back for the heroine he'd lost in the first film. Talk about a romantic movie.

"I think maybe you should wait for Morrigan," Mari was saying.

"Heroes don't wait. They act." He took a step toward the door but then turned back, not willing to miss this cinematic opportunity. "I'll be back."

CHAPTER TWO

"Give us a twirl, honey."

Rose Bishop grit her teeth at the gravelly voice. The casting director sounded as though he chewed day-old cigarettes instead of smoked them. He smelled like it too. The funk of burnt and mildewed tobacco made her empty stomach churn.

She wanted to say no but knew she couldn't. Her stomach was empty, and she needed the money from this photo shoot. Not to fill her stomach. To fill her prescription so that she could keep food down.

And so, Rose grounded her heel as she pivoted for his perverted gaze. In her mind, she imagined with relish that it was his twig of a dick that she was stomping and grinding as she turned to show the goods she had for sale.

Because that's what being a model was; putting your body, your looks on sale for others to either drape with clothing, cover with makeup, or strip you bare and display those same assets.

"Slow down," said Roy Gates, one such casting director that preferred the stripped bared assets of models.

Rose clenched her fists. She bit her tongue. Then she slowed her rotation so that Jail Bait Gates could get a good look at her ass. She didn't expect him to look too long since she'd stopped being jail bait nearly two years ago. And that's when the gigs had dried up for her and her sister.

"Hmmm," came the man's voice. There was no praise in it. Only disappointment.

Rose rolled her eyes all the way to the back of her head. She could do that now as she was still giving him the dark side of the moon. The joke was on him because all he got was a view of the long hem of her skirt. And by long, she meant that it fell to the midway part of her upper thigh.

"I don't know why she would come to casting dressed in that." The feminine voice was just as gravely and mildewed as Gates's but high pitched. It belonged to Park Palmer, the assistant casting director of Gateway Models.

More than male casting directors, Rose hated when women held the job. Park wrapped her thin lips around a vape and pulled. The gurgling sound brought to mind a cooing baby. Park Palmer was the furthest thing from maternal that a woman could get. She'd likely pimp out her own kid if the skinny twig of a woman could even muster the strength to carry a child.

Park put the vape down and rounded the table. Without permission or consent, she reached for the edge of Rose's skirt and hiked it up. Her acrylic nails scratched against Rose's skin as she folded the hem up twice, and then a third time until the new crease just touched Rose's butt cheek.

Rose clenched her fingers and pursed her lips. There was nothing she could say or do to keep her modesty and also get this job. Looked like the price of the job would be a bit of a moon.

Too bad the assistant wasn't done there. Next, Park reached for the straps of Rose's sensible top and pulled them down and around her shoulder caps. Thankfully, no nipples were revealed in the slutting up of her outfit.

"Better," drawled Gates. "But I'm still not seeing it."

Not seeing it? What more did he need? A nip slip? Proof of a thigh gap?

Oh, how Rose hated her career. But it wasn't like she had any other talents than her pretty face and a body that couldn't hold food down without medication. It was the need for that medication that brought her here today, readying to put her sick body on display.

Rose looked over at the couch in the corner, the casting couch. Part of her wanted to walk over and lay down. For a rest, not a fuck. She was so weary that she probably wouldn't notice if Jail Bait tried to mount her.

But if she let him have his way with her, she wouldn't be able to get the medication to keep her food down. And she needed the food in order to keep her body going. So she gave herself a shake and put on her prettiest smile.

"Nope." Gates gave a decisive shake of his head.

Models heard no on a daily basis in this business. So, the response wasn't a shock. What was were Gates' next words.

"She's pretty, but she looks nothing like her."

Rose glanced at the woman standing beside her.

She could've been looking into a mirror. Same fiery red hair. Same honey-golden skin. Only the other woman's skirt was higher up her thighs. Her cleavage was more on display. But her gaze was vacant as she wore the plastic smile the two of them had developed when they were just twelve years old and being sent on their first casting call.

"How can they not look the same?" said Park. "They're twins."

Gates looked between Rose and her sister Lily. Rose gritted her teeth to try and affect Lily's smile. But she could never get it right. Though they were identical, it was the one way their mother could always tell them apart. Mom always said Lily came out of the womb agreeable, never complaining. Whereas Rose wailed right after she took her first breath.

"They developed different," said Gates. "That one has bigger tits."

Gates pointed to Lily. Lily continued to look straight ahead. Staring at the wall. Placid smile still firmly in place.

Using her index finger, Park tugged at Lily's top and peered down. Then she turned to Rose, finger outstretched.

Rose glared at the offensive digit. Before she

could tell the woman exactly where she could put that finger, Rose heard a growl.

It wasn't her belly. It was Lily's. Neither of them had been able to hold anything down for nearly a week. Not since their last dose of their medication. And even that, they'd cut in half and shared.

Food was cheap. Their medication for gastroparesis was not. The rare disease caused the nerves in their stomach to become overly sensitive. That sensitivity slowed their digestion. Often making them feel full when they weren't. At other times, vomiting what little food they were able to consume and trying to keep down.

A cynical person would've called the disease a model's dream. A natural born reason that would keep them slim. The truth was, they were both undernourished and desperate for sustenance.

Which meant Rose couldn't slap away the assistant's hand. Not if she wanted to get herself and her sister fed anytime soon. Already, she could see Lily sway as she held tight to her smile and concentrated on the wall. Rose needed to do the same.

It took everything in Rose to hold still and let this happen. She had to let it happen. So, she pulled on a smile and pulled at the front of her top so that Park could get a peek inside.

"I can't see," said Gates. "Why don't you both take your tops off."

Rose tasted the bile at the back of her throat. The forced smile she was trying to hold onto fell completely. A glance in her peripheral vision told her that Lily had already moved past considering it and was moving toward action.

Lily caught her gaze. They had that twin thing where they knew what each other was thinking. They needed the money. They needed the medication. It was just their bodies. Neither of them had ever actually laid down on any couch. Because they usually took jobs together and therefore were never alone.

It was just their bodies. They needed the money. They needed their medication.

Rose could hear the last three phrases loudly in her sister's gaze. She heard when Lily flicked the button on her top. Rose reached out her hand to stay her sister's before she could get to the next button.

"Fine," said Gates. "You don't want to play ball, Rose? Get out. Lily can stay."

Lily gulped. They never allowed themselves to be separated. Another growl tore through the room. It wasn't Rose's belly. By the look of surprise on Lily's face, it wasn't hers either.

"You know what's worse than a man who takes advantage of a woman?" said a voice from the window. "A woman who takes advantage of other women."

They all turned to the woman in the window and gaped. Gaped because they were on the fourth floor of the office building. So how could anyone be at the window?

A woman in a figure-hugging leather suit stepped over the ledge in a pair of boots that Rose would've considered trading her meds for. Had this model casting call somehow turned into a call for actresses? Were they possibly being considered as a double for this woman? Because if so, neither Rose nor Lily would make the cut.

The woman was built like a brick house. She had curves where the twins were flat. Her full head of purple hair had to be a wig, an expensive one at that. And the muscles the woman had on her had to have come from testosterone injections. Though Rose had heard of plastic surgery where they sewed boob implants under the skin to look like muscle.

However, Rose got the distinct impression that this actress wasn't on call. If she was, why was Park backing up from her with fear in her eyes? Why had

Gates scrambled out of his chair and back to the wall?

"There's a cold place in hell for a woman like you," the purple-haired action star was saying. "Unfortunately, I can't give you a ride. I'm here for them."

Unnaturally bright eyes shone a spotlight on Rose and Lily. Rose turned her body, trying to shield her baby sister. Though they had shared a womb and were born on the same day, Rose was a full hour older. A fact she never let Lily forget.

"Wherever there's trouble, I always seem to find a fireblood." She turned her back on the two predators and walked toward Rose and Lily. That was her first mistake. Never give your back to a casting director.

Two things happened at once. Park made a dash for the door. While Gates pulled a gun out of the drawer.

For a second, Rose wondered if she was hallucinating. Sometimes when the nausea and abdominal pain hit, her mind wandered, and she saw things. Things like fire dancing in the sunlight. Flowers lifting up their petals and whispering to her. She'd never told anyone about these visions, not even Lily.

So when Lily pulled Rose to the ground a split

second before the gun went off, Rose knew she wasn't hallucinating. Gates really had just pulled a gun and shot it. Pain radiated through Rose's frail, malnourished body. But she'd live. There were no holes in either her or Lily. The only impact that had hit them was their bodies on the floor.

"I hate guns," said the purple-haired woman. "Trust a man to invent something phallic to shoot a seed that kills."

Rose looked up to find the woman eyeing the bullet as she turned it over in her hand. Smoke still billowed from the barrel where the bullet had shot from. Had she caught the bullet?

No. That was impossible. Rose decided she needed to revisit the idea of hallucinations again. Especially when the purple-haired woman cocked her arm back like a pitcher tossing a ball and let the bullet fly.

Park, whose hand had been on the doorknob, screamed and crumpled to the floor. Blood oozed from a hole in her hand. That woman had just thrown the bullet at the fleeing assistant with the velocity of a firearm.

It was settled. Rose was delirious from the lack of sustenance in her belly. Because the other explanation simply wasn't possible. When she looked over at her sister, Rose knew through the twin connection that Lily had seen the unbelievable feat as well.

"I'll be back for the two of you someday," said the purple-haired woman. Then she turned to look down at Rose and Lily. "You two, you're coming with me."

Then Rose was airborne. She was being tossed out a window. Her scream caught in her throat because when she looked down and didn't see the ground she was expecting to see, her eyes rolled back in her head. Because she couldn't have seen what she thought she had just seen. She couldn't have seen a dragon floating outside the window with its wings outstretched and a friendly smile on its face.

That was the last thing she remembered before blackness took her.

CHAPTER THREE

Ilia pushed his body to slice faster through the air currents. His dark scales, a purple so deep it could be the black of the sky, blended with the night. His wingspan so vast that he covered the distance quickly. Birds gave him a wide berth.

As a fledgling, he'd been slow to fly. His paper-thin wings hadn't had enough strength to carry his small, weak body. Now, Ilia was the strongest creature on land or in the air.

He flew with a purpose. His movements agile and precise as he covered the distance to the Veil, that crack in the atmosphere that was the boundary between the garden the Goddess cordoned off to experiment on life and the world beyond where she let her favorite experiments roam free and procreate.

There wasn't much procreation going on on this side of the Veil. The forgotten early trials of the Goddess had everlasting life but not the ability to breed. Her daughters, the Valkyrie, were born fully-fledged warriors who could take life, but they were sterile—and largely uninterested—when it came to creating it. She had crafted beasts who could shift their shape into men. But she had not made a single female who could do the same. The only beings on this side of the Veil who could beget life were the fae-kind. However, their way of *doing it* didn't seem to Ilia to be all that fun.

Ilia wasn't interested in fairies anymore. The only female he wanted was the one that would be his, and his alone. She was near.

He could feel it in his bones. He could hear her in his chest. She needed him. He wouldn't fail her. He would be her hero.

Ilia pushed himself even harder. The flapping of his wings like a drumbeat in the night. His breaths a rumble of thunder on the horizon. Everything got out of his way as he flew. Until one thing didn't.

Ilia was not the only apex predator in the air. A golden-brown light streaked across the sky, like sunlight flashing into the night. Ilia groaned as he reduced his speed and came in for a landing. His descent was smooth. So was the golden dragon's.

With a crunch of bone and sinew, both he and his brother shifted from their dragon state. Ilia's dragon resisted the shift at first. Both man and beast could sense that she was near. For the first time, Ilia had to fight his dragon for control of his body.

He'd watched his other brothers struggle with their beasts over the years. Without a human female to take as a mate, the dragons slowly gained control over the men. Beryl had been the least in control until he claimed Poppy. Rhoyl had given up entirely. None of them had seen Rhoyl as a man for years.

With a grunt and shove, Ilia reclaimed his body from the dragon. He straightened on powerful thighs that had once been too feeble to hold his form. It took Elek a moment longer to shift. Unlike the rest of his brothers, Elek didn't spend much time in his dragon form. The human part of him was always in total control.

"Where are you headed?" Elek said.

"The Veil." Ilia began walking the rest of the way. Already he could feel the surge of power from the rift between worlds. The energy was hot, but it gave off no actual heat. Just a feeling that he would burn from the inside out if he got too close. Ilia kept moving forward.

"Are you expecting a delivery from Morrigan?" Elek asked, close on his heels.

"No. I'm going to get my package myself."

Elek's steps didn't falter, but he did fall a step behind Ilia. Ilia felt his brother's steady gaze on his back. Of all his brothers, he was the least happy to have Elek follow him.

Corun would've used logic to deter him from his mission. Kimber would've shouted a command to turn around. Beryl would've tried to step in front of Ilia to get there first.

But Elek? He caught up with Ilia. Not getting in front of him. Not lagging behind him. Elek simply nodded his head with no other comment.

Ilia came to a halt and faced his brother. "What?"

Elek raised a brow. "What what?"

"You think it's impulsive? You think I'm making a mistake?"

"Do you feel you're making an impulsive mistake?"

This is why Ilia wished another of his brothers had followed him. Elek's nonjudgmental attitude always appeared to Ilia as a mirror. With no discrimination, Elek acted as a reflection of one's emotions.

"Come with me," Ilia said, changing tactics.

"Come with you beyond the Veil?"

"Yes. To find our mates."

"I don't want a mate," said Elek.

"You're going to need a mate if you want to stay a man," Ilia insisted.

"If the dragon takes me," Elek shrugged, "so be it. I can do my work in either form."

"Then do it for Rhoyl. He's lost to us, but if we find his mate, he might come back."

"Rhoyl's not lost," said Elek. "He made a choice."

See? It was just like talking to a mirror. Or worse, a puddle of muddy water that made no sense.

"Well, I'm going in," said Ilia, turning away from his brother and back to that hot wave of energy. "I'll be like Arnold in the *Terminator* movies looking for our Sarah Connor."

"Didn't the Terminator go to kill Sarah Connor?"

Why did everyone see the movie that way? Ilia didn't want to waste time explaining the plot. He could feel her near. His very own Sarah.

"Besides, that's a fictional story, brother," Elek continued. "That is the real world out there, not a film. You can't survive there."

"I won't be there long," said Ilia. "I have a plan. I'll find Arnold, and he'll help me."

"The Terminator isn't real, Ilia."

"Arnold is real. Chryssie said he's a governor now. I'll find a phone box, call Governor Schwarzenegger, and then we'll look in the Book of Yellow Pages and find my mate. Easy."

Elek sighed. But at least he didn't argue any longer. How could he argue? Ilia's plan was solid. This would work.

The heat radiating off that tear in the fabric of the Earth pushed at Ilia. But Ilia had met bigger and meaner bullies. He pushed back.

Even with all the strength he'd gained from years of fighting wasn't enough. The Veil blasted outward, sending both Ilia and Elek back on their bare asses.

When Ilia was able to open his eyes, he saw a dragon emerge. It sailed through the crack to land a few feet from Ilia. The dragon was a natural-born beast who didn't harbor a man inside of him. This dragon had a woman on his back.

"Oh good, you two are here. That saves me a trip."

Morrigan slid a leg over the dragon's back and dismounted. Then she reached up and grabbed first one and then another sack. She tossed the first to Ilia. Elek caught the other.

The sacks weren't heavy. They were light as a bouquet of flowers. In fact, the sacks smelled like the most fragrant blossoms Ilia had ever come in contact with. They smelled like human women.

"These are the last two with fire in their blood," said Morrigan. "Now that I've cleaned up that little mess Draco and Regin made by letting the pregnant human back across the Veil, I'm done being your dating app. Have a nice life."

And with that, Morrigan hopped back on board her dragon and took flight. Ilia and Elek watched her fly off. Then they both looked down at what they held in their arms.

Ilia pulled the covering off the sack. Inside, he found a heart-shaped face surrounded by hair like fire. Two pink lips that looked ready to be kissed. And pale skin that appeared translucent under the moon's light.

Elek removed the sack covering to reveal an identical face. Twins. They had been delivered as twins.

And one of them was Ilia's. He felt it in his bones, in his heart. But which one?

"I have dibs," Ilia said.

CHAPTER FOUR

ose knew she was sleeping. She felt warm and toasty in her bed. Like she was floating on a cloud, not the hard mattress she shared with her sister. Her body was stretched, and her muscles felt languid. Her belly was full and settled. Not a grumble or twinge of pain to be found.

This dream was heaven. More than anything, she did not want to wake from this fantasy. It was better than any reality.

Still, something urged her to open her eyes. It wasn't a sense of danger. Not like when she was in a dressing room on a modeling gig and a picture frame was askew because it held a hidden camera. Not like when she was on set, and the photographer asked her to put on and take off a robe when Rose could see the continuous red light on the camera that indicated it was recording a video he could later use on a porn site.

No. Rose didn't feel she was in that kind of danger. She felt exposed, but she also felt no need to cover up. She knew without knowing how she knew that her body was protected from any harm or leering eyes.

Though the dreamworld was heaven, Rose knew that back in reality, she could be in danger. There was silence in her bedroom. There was never silence in her bedroom.

Normally, she could hear the next-door neighbors arguing. The woman screeching, followed by the thud of flesh against flesh. Sometimes that thudding was carnal. Most times, it was the thud of violence, followed by the sirens of police.

But Rose didn't remember making it home. The last thing she remembered was being at the casting call for the latest modeling gig with her sister. She remembered Park tugging at her clothes to reveal more of her skin. She remembered Gates ogling at her with those beady eyes of his. And then blackness.

Oh, no. What if she had been drugged? Again.

That had to be the reason for the warm toasty feeling and the blessed silence. Coupled with how loose her body felt. Those bastards had drugged her.

But how? She didn't remember drinking or eating anything. They hadn't offered. And even if they had, she knew better than to take it.

Still, something wasn't quite right. Mainly because everything felt right. Rose felt safe, and warm, and comfortable. Such unfamiliar feelings that assured her that she was, indeed, in grave danger.

Rose struggled to open first one then another eyelid. When she managed to slit her eyes open a fraction, she wished she'd closed them back. A bright purple light assaulted her eyes.

It was like Barney, the purple dinosaur, had his butt in her face. The jewel-tone shimmered like the giant stuffed animal was twerking right under her nose. Rose had never seen anything like it.

Her eyes quickly adjusted, and she opened them wider to see that there was no purple dinosaur. This wasn't an actual light. There were gems all around her.

Were these jade? Amethyst? Rose didn't know her jewels. She'd never worn anything except loaned jewelry on-set or costume jewelry bought at the convenience store. She knew that what she was seeing all around her was the real deal.

Where the hell was she?

Actually, no. Scratch that. Rose became less concerned with where she was and more concerned with why she couldn't move.

She looked up to see that her forearms were bound with rope. She knew she should panic. But a different feeling won the race up her arms and into her chest.

Fascination.

Rose was fascinated by the intricate knots along her forearms. The rope was the same deep shade of purple as the gems. Where the three knots formed, they bloomed out to make loops that reminded her of rose petals.

Looking down, she saw the same patterns over her legs. In the past, on runways and on photo shoots, she had been dressed in the most bizarre of costumes, from strips of paper to aluminum foil. But never rope. Never something that constricted her movement.

That's when she remembered; she couldn't move. She wasn't being dressed up. She was being held against her will.

Now the panic moved in. Rose struggled against

the ropes to break free. The instant she tried to free herself, pain slammed into her.

Abrasions from the bindings scratched at her arms where they had cradled her only a second ago. The cords tightened where they were fastened and dug into her skin.

Rose stopped moving. The moment she did, the relief was instant and all-consuming. Pleasure replaced the pain.

Her mind reeled at the opposite reactions. She held still, and that languid feeling cascaded through her body once more. When she struggled, she felt pain. When she relaxed, she felt like she never needed to move again.

What the actual hell?

Beside her, Rose heard a moan. The moan was sleepy but pleasure-filled. She craned her neck to see that her sister hung beside her. Same dark purple ropes. Same blooming roses at the knots.

Seeing her sister bound like that had Rose seeing red. She tugged again at the ropes, uncaring of the pain. A sound alerted her to movement to the side. It was a tinkling sound, like nails tapping against the dinner table.

Darkness separated itself from pitch black. Rose thought she made out a pair of wings. But no bird's wings were large enough to span that width, the size of two cars parked side by side.

The wings folded inward with a snap. The sound reminded Rose of an umbrella folding. The large, lizard-like body gave itself a shake as though it was shaking off dew drops.

Rose could only gape as she stared. Then memories hit her.

The purple-haired woman with the kickass boots.

The gun held in Gates's shaky hands.

The bullet tossed at Park as she ran.

The dragon smiling at Rose as she was flung out of a window.

Dragon.

Rose stared at the dark form. She blinked, and the dragon was gone. Standing before her was a man. A tall man with more muscles than any body-builder she'd ever seen. Shoulders that looked like boulders. Thighs that looked like tree trunks. And a third leg that…

No. That wasn't a leg. That appendage was what made Rose avert her gaze and continue her struggle.

"Stop. You'll hurt yourself."

Rose stilled at the sound of that deep voice. Just like the ropes that sent pleasure through her when she let them hold her still, the man's voice sent the same bliss-filled waves down to the core of her body. Rose told her loins and the burgeoning Stockholm Syndrome to fuck off.

"Hey." The naked man waved his hands in a friendly manner that had no place in this kidnapping. "I'm your new brother."

"What?" said Rose, her voice quaking so much on the single word that she barely heard herself.

"Yes," the naked man grinned. "Welcome to the family."

"What?" Rose's voice gained enough traction that time to carry around the room.

That's when Lily opened her eyes. Her sister's gaze went wide as she took in the scene; her bound hands, the naked man. And then Lily screamed so loud, so violently, that the man covered his ears. Once the last gust of air left Lily, she promptly passed out again.

"Would you look at that," said the naked man with a grin that looked smitten. "A true damsel in distress. I'm going to be her hero."

CHAPTER FIVE

Ilia had a mate. Finally. After waiting dutifully in line behind his older brothers when they'd all agreed to be gentlemen about mating. Then trying to cut in front by using his fists when they'd gone back on their word. Only to give his brothers the benefit of the doubt once more when they'd agreed to his dibs.

It had all worked out in the end. He had a mate. And she was perfect.

Looking down at her lovely form, Ilia wondered if this is what his hero Arnold felt like when he'd won Mr. Olympia for the first time. Ilia certainly felt like he was a mountain in comparison to his mate. Where he was boulders and crags, she was branches and twigs.

Her slender limbs were a little too fine. There was no bruising on her wrist where the ropes met flesh. Because his mate was more bone than flesh.

He saw the protrusions of her carpus as he unbound her hands. Her skin was pale, more porcelain than the golden tan he was used to seeing in Chryssie, Poppy, and Cardi.

Although Cardi had looked very sick when she'd first arrived. But after Cardi had opened her eyes and then her mouth, the little spitfire quickly brightened and filled out, much to Kimber's dismay.

Ilia was certain his mate would do the same once she woke up. She'd probably shine brighter than Cardi and put on more weight. All of which Ilia would love to see happen. Despite only having fairies in his bed, he had always been attracted to the fairer sex that had a little extra meat on their bones.

Looking over at his mate's twin, he noted that she was only slightly more meaty. The twin had bruises on her wrists. Unlike Ilia's mate, the sister had struggled. She was struggling still as she hurled every manner of foul word at Ilia as he surveyed his bride-to-be.

"Only a man with a carrot for a dick would ever need to kidnap a woman to get his kicks."

"A carrot?" asked Ilia. "Those are quite long, you know. And firm."

"And skinny. And breakable with a good crunch of the jaw."

Ilia spared his soon-to-be sister-in-Goddess a glance. Upon his second perusal, he realized she looked nothing like his mate. There was a wildness in her eyes. Her flushed skin was more pink than porcelain, like she had fire waiting to shoot out of her veins and burn him.

"I didn't kidnap you," he said, cradling his mate's lolling head in the crook of his arm. "That was the Valkyrie."

Ilia returned his attention to his mate. Though her frame was frail, her proportions were bountiful. Her waist was slender, but her hips were round and full, a good size for breeding.

"Morrigan didn't kidnap you," he continued. "She saved you. You both have fire in your blood. You would not have lived long beyond the Veil."

Trails of red veins snaked across his mate's chest, leading his eyes to her breasts. They appeared to be handfuls. The swell of them peeked from the bust line of her threadbare shirt.

"If you touch her, I will cut off your balls with a spoon."

Inside his body, Ilia's dragon sat up on its haunches. "A spoon? You know that has no sharp edges."

"Exactly," the twin hissed. "A very, very dull spoon."

His dragon found that funny. Ilia did too. Like all dragons, he found violence fetching. This woman would be fun to tussle around with.

As a sister.

Not as a mate.

Ilia had already chosen his mate.

From the corner of his eyes, Ilia noted that the twin sister's breasts weren't as full as his mate's. That was curious that they would have been born with that particular disparity. Luckily, he'd chosen the bountiful twin. The more beautiful twin.

His mate was the Allison of the two. The nerdy girl who was a shadow next to Claire, the popular girl in the great film *The Breakfast Club*. Bender, the hero of that film, ended up with the popular girl. And if there was a hero, other than the Terminator, then it was Bender. And it was Claire for Bender. So it was the lovelier sister for Ilia.

"What's her name?" he asked.

"Last name, You. First name, Fuck."

Again, a chuckle escaped Ilia's lips. "We're going

to get along very well, little sister. What's your name?"

"Are you a crazy person?"

"I'm not a person. I'm a dragon."

She gulped. Her pale eyes went hazy, as though in remembrance of something unpleasant. She had spent most of her life not knowing that his kind existed. All in one night, she had met at least two dragons.

She must be frightened. He should probably unbind her. Though he didn't want to let his mate go.

"My name is Ilia. I promise no one will hurt you."

"Yeah? Kinda hard to believe with the being tied up and held against my will by a… whatever you are."

She paused then. Looking up at her bound hands. Then back down at him.

"You're the dragon I saw," she said. "Aren't you."

Ilia nodded.

"Are we dead? Is this hell?"

"No. I already told you, you're beyond the Veil. You're safe."

"I repeat," she motioned to her hands, "tied up."

"This is all ritual. It must be done."

"Ritual for what? Are you going to turn back into a dragon again and eat me?"

Ilia's blood boiled as the words left her lips. They kept playing in his head on a loop. *Are you going to eat me?*

His dragon liked the idea. He very much wanted to spend the rest of the evening laying between a woman's warm thighs and lapping at her flesh. *Are you going to eat me?*

He gave his head a shake. He wasn't going to eat that woman. She was going to be his sister. He was going to eat the woman in his arms.

He looked down at his mate. She looked even paler than before. It shouldn't take her this long to wake up. She felt cool to the touch. Ilia wondered if he should be concerned?

Then her lips parted. "Rose?"

Both Ilia and his dragon stilled at the sound of his mate's voice. It was lower than he had expected. Low and raspy, as though she consumed a blaze that had scorched her throat.

"Rose? Are you there?"

"I'm here, Lily. Everything's going to be fine."

Ilia didn't spare Rose another glance. But he could tell that she was struggling against the ropes again.

"Hello, Lily," Ilia said. "My name is Ilia."

Lily gaped at him. Her pale eyes wide with incomprehension. Her thin lips rounding in a quivering O.

Before Ilia could continue to assure her, a great whoosh crackled against the walls of the underground cavern. Ilia looked up to see his brother Rhoyl descend in a blaze of blue wings and scales.

Lily's eyes widened impossibly larger, making Ilia worry that she might break a nerve in her head. Beside them, Rose pulled and yanked at the ropes which still bound her.

"That's my brother. Don't be frightened."

Rhoyl came into the light. His scales gleamed. A scream tore through the room. Ilia shouldn't have worried over the frailness of his mate, not with that set of pipes on her.

No sooner than Lily's earsplitting cry started did it stop. She fainted in his arms. Eyes closed, mouth slack, and body limp.

Ilia sighed and turned to Rose, who had managed to slip one of her thin wrists out of his ties and was working on another. Since Ilia wouldn't be able to complete the bonding ritual with his mate incapacitated, he sat Lily down and went over to Rose to began the process of cutting her down.

But the moment he came near her, she cocked her fist back and landed a punch to his nose. It didn't hurt. Not with her being such a wee thing. Still, it was a jolt. It felt like her love tap knocked something loose inside him.

When he looked at Rose again, it was as though scales had fallen from his eyes. There was a glow to her. One that had the dragon peering out of his eyes to gape at her.

Ilia had found a mate just in time. He was quickly loosening the leash he had on his dragon. Because though his mate lay a few feet away from him on the floor, his incisors were sharpening to take a bite out of her sister.

CHAPTER SIX

ose was slow to come to wakefulness this time. She dreamed of fire and bondage. Of dark scales and warm flesh. Of sharp teeth and sensual lips. It should've been a nightmare, but she was aroused in her sleep. Which meant it had to be a dream.

Rose was no shrinking virgin. One thing she knew for certain was that sex had been invented by men for men. It certainly wasn't for women.

The romance novels and porn videos lured women in with talk of crashing waves and sounds of enthusiastic moans. If women only read the words closely, they would be horrified at the adjectives describing throbbing parts of the male anatomy coming anywhere near their flowers. If they looked closely at the readily available porn on the internet, they would see women more concerned with their hairstyles and camera placement than the thrusting action going on down below.

Sex was awful. Painful. And entirely one-sided. It was women who had their flesh bruised and torn by a man's quivering member. Which was why Rose was adamant that she was never doing that again.

Not even in her dreams. She gave a mental shake to douse the fire and loosen the imaginary knots binding her hands. She brushed away the scales and slapped at the flesh. She gnashed her teeth, ready to bite any lips that came near her, even if inside her head.

With that, she was able to fling her eyes open. She expected to be confronted with the creatures from her nightmares; the dragons. Because apparently, dragons were a real thing in the real world. A fact that she would just have to freak out about later. Right now, it was self-preservation. She had to get herself and her sister out of this madness.

With her eyes open, Rose didn't see any scaly-clawed, sharp-toothed males looking down at her. She was in a room full of women. All red-haired women who looked at her with eager expressions.

"Don't crowd her, Cardi," said a woman with

vibrant red hair that was braided in a plait that hung over one shoulder. "Give her some space to breathe."

"She's breathing just fine," said the woman beside her, who Rose assumed was Cardi.

Cardi's hair was teased high with curls that didn't bounce. That amount of non-bouncy curls could only be tamed with a can and a half of hairspray. Rose caught the unmistakable smell of Aqua Net in the air and sneezed. Cardi looked like she was on her way into a mall during the 80s to see a boy band who was opening for Tiffany or Debbie Gibson.

"Hi, I'm Cardi. This is Chryssie, and this is Poppy."

Poppy, another redhead with springy curls that were relaxed around her heart-shaped face, stood behind the other two redheads. She gave Rose a shy smile and a little wave.

Rose's gaze went from one woman to the other. Each woman looked different. But at the same time, they looked like the other.

It was more than their hair color. Redheads weren't rare. However, most had pale skin to accompany their hair. These three women had tan to caramel skin like Rose and her sister.

Well, like Rose and Lily's skin had been when

they were well-nourished. During the days when they booked enough modeling gigs that they could afford their medication to keep their bellies full. These days, with their stomachs rejecting anything that came down their throats, both of their skin looked as paper-white as it felt paper-thin.

"Which one are you?" asked Cardi. "Rose or Lily?"

Rose looked beside her to see Lily coming awake on the same plush couch that she sat on. Rose grabbed her sister by the shoulders.

"Lil? You okay?" Rose asked as she ran her hands up and down her sister's body. She expected to feel the persistent slight chill on her sister's skin that came from malnourishment. It was one of the body's defense mechanisms against their disease. When there wasn't enough sustenance, it slowed all processes down to conserve energy.

Lily's skin was warm. There was also color to her cheeks that hadn't been there in months, maybe a whole year. Lily looked well, healthy. As if she'd gotten in a full meal and held it down.

"Oh, Rose," Lily sighed. "I had the worst nightmare. You wouldn't even believe it."

"It's not a nightmare, Lils. It's real."

Rose didn't need to look at her twin to see the

realization and horror darken her eyes. She felt it in the stiffening of Lily's posture as they both turned to face the women. Rose was on high alert, trying to determine if these three were friend or foe. It wouldn't be the first time men sent out members of the fairer sex to do their dirty work.

"Hi-eee, Lily," said Cardi. "It's so totally radical to meet you."

Not only was the woman an 80's fashion reject, she was also a connoisseur of the slang. Now Rose's ears hurt as much as her eyes.

Rose's eyes only counted two women. Where was the third? The redhead with the soft curls around her face.

Rose spotted Poppy across the room. She was putting items on a plate and then one directly in her mouth. The smell of the food reached Rose from her place on the couch, and her mouth watered.

"You notice how they have flower names, just like us?" said Chryssie. "My full name is Chrysanthemum. I guess all our mothers got the memo."

"What is she talking about?" Lily said to Rose. "I want to get out of here."

Rose heard the fear in her sister's voice. But that wasn't the sense that was heightened at the moment.

It was her sense of smell. Was that chocolate she smelled?

Rose had never hungered for chocolate in her entire life. The treat had very little nourishment, so she would never waste the precious space in her stomach for something with so little nutrition. But the scent of the chocolate lifted her head. Just like in cartoons where the scent-waves lifted a character up by the nostrils and made them float toward the plate.

"You guys actually are home," said Cardi, coming to sit on the edge of the couch. The tulle of her skort spilled glitter onto Rose's leg. "This is where you come from. Well, where your ancestor came from; way, way back in the sixties."

"It was the seventies, Cardi," said Chryssie.

"That's still a long, long time ago." Cardi waved her comment away with a flourish of what had to be Lee Press-On Nails. "Anywho, she shacked up with a dragon—"

"The rumor is she had sex with two dragon brothers," said Chryssie.

"Then she went back across the Veil and had a half-dragon, half-human baby who was our ancestor."

Rose listened to this story. Her head swinging

back and forth from Chryssie to Cardi as they volleyed this tall tale. Finally, her gaze came to rest on Poppy, who had a dollop of rich, dark chocolate on her thumb.

"It's true," said Poppy, after licking away the ooey-gooey dessert. "We're all the descendants of dragons. That's why I would break out in spots on the other side."

"I had an abundance of helium in my blood," said Chryssie. "It gave me constant fatigue, cold intolerance, and shortness of breath."

"They thought I had cancer," said Cardi. "It all cleared up when we came on this side of the Veil because we weren't meant to live in the human world. What's wrong with the two of you?"

"Cardi," hissed Chryssie. "That's rude."

"What?" shrugged Cardi. "We're family. And whatever they were sick with before doesn't matter anymore."

That brought Rose's attention away from the platter of food in Poppy's hand. But only for an instant. Gastroparesis had no cure. All they could do was manage the symptoms.

Except Rose wasn't feeling the normal chill in her blood. The fatigue that plagued her bones was surprisingly absent. Most surprising, her stomach grumbled. Not in rejection. That was hunger pains she was feeling.

"Where are my manners?" said Poppy. "You want some?"

Poppy held the plate out to Rose and Lily. Up close, the scent-wave slapped her in the face. Before Rose knew what she was doing, she reached out for one of the square treats.

Was this a brownie? Rose had never had a brownie before. It went down her throat with the same ease as a kid slipping down a sliding board on a warm summer's day.

She felt the food pass down her chest and work its way lower. She froze in fear as its descent continued. Any moment now, her stomach muscles would become uncoordinated, and the food would come back up.

Except the clenching never came. What did come was a sugar rush so big and powerful that Rose saw a light so bright, she was certain she'd died, and this was heaven.

The food stayed down. Without any medicine. It was a miracle—one that Rose wasn't going to pass up.

She turned and handed a large square to Lily. Lily looked at the food warily. But the same scent wave must have slapped her in the face because she took a bite. And then another. There were tears in Lily's eyes when she looked back at her sister.

"I know what you're thinking," said Chryssie. "You're thinking you're dead. I thought that too. But you're not. You're back where you belong."

"You're beyond the Veil," said Cardi. "It's technically the Garden of Eden. A place where God—actually the Goddess—tinkered with her creations. Dragons are one of those creations, and you're part dragon."

Part dragon? Part angel? Part demon? Rose didn't care, so long as she could eat like a normal person. So long as she'd go through a day where her body wasn't attacking itself. And, hell, if she could have a brownie, then that was even better than having a cherry on top.

"What's the catch?" said Rose, grabbing another treat from Poppy's plate.

"You get to stay here in this castle," said Chryssie.

"You'll live longer than your normal human life, so long as you don't cross back over the Veil," said Cardi.

Rose licked her fingers, looking at each woman in turn. "The catch?"

Cardi wet her glossy lips and then bit down on

her bottom lip as she avoided their gazes. Chryssie tugged at the end of her ponytail, also while avoiding their gazes. Poppy turned back to the table to pile on more treats.

"It's going to sound worse than it actually is," Chryssie finally said.

CHAPTER SEVEN

"Why will no one respect my dibs?"

A plume of dark smoke accompanied Ilia's huff of indignation. He crossed his arms over his chest, his muscles bulging with tension. A few of the threads of fabric snapped at the move. His brothers were lucky he didn't snap at them with how tightly he was wound.

"Everyone heard Kimber say I have dibs on the next sacrifice," Ilia continued, pointing at each of his brothers in turn. "You're all nothing but douches if you don't respect the dibs."

"Do you even know what a douche is?" asked Corun.

"Yeah, I do." Ilia snapped his fingers, then cocked his thumb like a gun and his index finger like a barrel which pointed directly at Corun. "It's you if you go back on your word."

Corun hung his head in his hands and let out a sigh. The sigh didn't sound remorseful. Not like he was sorry for not recognizing Ilia's dibs. It sounded annoyed, which he didn't have any right to be. It was Ilia who was the wronged party here.

"Ilia," said Kimber, his deep voice resonate and sharp like the diamond gems he mined. "No one is questioning your dibs."

Ilia wanted to relax his posture. But he couldn't. His years of being a runt, of being the last in line and often cut off by their father, didn't allow him to let his guard down. Not even with his brothers when it came to a matter of getting what he was due.

"Neither Elek or Rhoyl will approach your potential mate."

"Potential?" growled Ilia, the muscles in his back bunching at the sound of that word. "Rose isn't potential anything. She's mine."

"I thought her name was Lily," said Corun.

"It is," said Ilia. "That's what I said."

"That's not what he said," Corun said to Kimber.

"The girls are twins," Kimber shrugged. "He may have gotten them confused."

"They're nothing alike," said Ilia. "Lily is beautiful. She looks like she's frail, but she has a strong set of lungs on her. Rose, on the other hand, Rose has a mouth on her. Her cheeks go red when she's angry, fire red like she's going to flame up. And she's funny. She called my dick a carrot and said she'd cut it off with a spoon. Can you believe that? And Rose is brave. If she hadn't been tied up, I'm sure she would've come at me. She did get in a shot. But her form was all wrong. And she barely has any strength. I'll need to teach her how to throw a punch when..."

Ilia trailed off when he noticed the looks Corun and Kimber kept sliding one another. His two older brothers had a habit of doing that; that silent communication between twins that Ilia had never managed with Beryl and Rhoyl. Because Ilia had always been shut out, cut off.

Well, not this time.

"I called dibs." Ilia only just managed not to stomp his foot for emphasis. That would've made him look like a fledgling throwing a tantrum.

"You have dibs," said Kimber. "You get time to woo... whichever female you choose to give your attentions to."

"Lily," said Ilia.

"Right. Lily." Kimber nodded. "But it's only a matter of time before the others find out."

The thought of the lions, or bears, or wolves getting a whiff of either of the girls set Ilia's molars to grinding. Neither Lily nor Rose belonged in a den or a cave. They were both princesses who belonged in a castle.

Though he suspected Rose would probably insist on being a lady knight, like Sarah Connor in the second Terminator film. He could just imagine Rose in a black t-shirt with her hair pulled back in a ponytail, aviator glasses shielding her gaze, while an automatic rifle was slung over her shoulder.

"She has to choose you," Kimber was saying.

"Who?" asked Ilia.

Once again, Kimber and Corun exchanged one of those silent, twin looks.

"Whichever one you and your dragon chooses to mate. Even though we all agree you have dibs, she has to choose you. And she has to do it before the others find out they're here."

"She'll choose me," Ilia said. Of course, she would choose him. She was a damsel, and he was a hero. They were meant to be; all the storybooks, movies, and video games said so.

"Which one?" Corun asked.

"What do you mean, which one? Lily, of course." Ilia's belly grumbled as he made the last statement. Either he was hungry, or his dragon wanted to get to his woman sooner rather than later. He turned to leave but then hesitated. "What about Rose?"

"What about her?" asked Corun, a brow raised in the way when he had just worked out a complex mathematical problem that no one else had a clue about.

"We can't let one of the others get their hands on her," said Ilia. "She's our family. She's a fireblood. And I'm sure Lily won't want to stay if she's gone."

"Maybe she'll choose Elek or Rhoyl," said Kimber.

Ilia pursed his lips. He couldn't imagine that spitfire of a woman with quiet and contemplative Elek, who preferred to spend his time in the kitchens cooking or in the room with his comatose mother. But neither could he see Rose with Rhoyl, who had refused to shift back into male form for many years now.

Rose wasn't a problem Ilia could solve at the moment. He had to first focus on his mate. He had to convince Lily that he was her hero. Otherwise, she might be carted off by other beasts.

CHAPTER EIGHT

So this was the catch. Hang out with the dragons to see if she might find one of them attractive enough to date. Yeah, like that would ever happen.

It didn't matter if they had balls or scales, Rose wasn't attracted to men of any species. Not that she was attracted to women. She just wasn't into sex. And that's all men wanted was to look at naked women and pinch them in their soft and squishy places.

No, thank you, and fuck off. That's what she had to say to that.

"Yes, please," she said to Elek as he handed her another treat.

It was a meat of some sort. Rose hadn't bothered to

question what species. Not when it fell off the bone and slid down her throat, all while bursting with spicy flavors she had never been able to stomach. She saw stars as she closed her eyes, hummed, and took another bite. It could be made of fairies for all she cared.

Wait? Were fairies real? Probably if dragons were.

Elek, the dragon, placed a helping of a colorful food on her plate next. It looked like a flower. It tasted like heaven. Rose was getting perilously close to offering the man-beast anything he wanted if he kept filling her belly like this.

"That's called Nanjinganthus Dendrostyla," said Elek. "It's an angiosperm that's over one hundred million years old. It was the first flowering plant."

Rose waited for the dirty joke about her eating sperm. It didn't come. Which would've been another joke. Elek turned back to open a pit stove and stirred some other delectable ingredients into a pot. Rose shoved the angiosperm into her mouth and swallowed.

Man, if any homosapien could hear what was going on in her head, he would have a field day. Maybe dragons were different?

Rose licked her fingers clean of the plant's juices.

It was the third dish she'd tried, not including the three brownies she'd scarfed down. And every morsel stayed in her belly. There wasn't a grumble to be heard from the organ.

However, she did hear a rumbling growl. She felt a squeezing contraction. In her throat, there was a gnawing need. As if everything inside her were crying out for more.

These were hunger pangs. A sensation she'd only read about because she had felt an empty-fullness in her stomach all her life. Now, not only was Rose hungry, she could do something about it that didn't involve careful meal planning after a dose of medication.

Really, she might actually contemplate sleeping with Elek if he could make her belly feel this good.

"So, this is the catch?" she said around a mouthful of the as yet unidentified meat.

"You mean one of the games with a ball?" asked Elek as he gave a pan a shake.

"Game, yes. But with your balls."

"My balls?"

"You want me to play with your balls in exchange for this food, right?" Rose pointed at his package, which was covered by a pair of cotton pants and an apron with the words *Your Opinion Was Not In The Recipe* across his chest.

Elek looked down at his groin area, then back at her. A quizzical expression furrowed his dark brows. "Why would I want that?"

"Because you're a man. And all men want sex."

"I'm not wholly a man. I'm part dragon. Also, I'm not interested in sex."

Rose sat back and gaped. In the silence that ensued, she heard the pop of oil in the pan. The sizzle of more meat and flowers cooking. And the grinding of bone under teeth.

In the corner sat the blue scaled dragon. Rhoyl was his name. He had yet to change into his human form. But his expressions were strangely human-like. Rhoyl had devoured the meat of the dish and was now finishing off the bone. He looked up at Rose, and a grin spread over his elongated face.

"So, he wants sex?" Rose asked, pointing to the dragon.

A furrow developed between the dragon's brows, making him look like an indignant devil.

"I don't think so," said Elek. "Even if he did, I don't think that would be safe for a woman to forni-cate with him in that form. Or sanitary."

Now both the man and the beast were studying Rose with disconcerting expressions. As though she, the one who kept inside her skin and didn't shift into another species, was the oddball in this scenario.

"No, it's not me," said Rose, waving her hands. "I don't want to have sex. You're males. You're the ones with dirty minds."

Rhoyl let out a huff and went back to his bone.

Elek raised a brow and went back to his stirring. "The food is free, no strings or balls attached. Neither Rhoyl nor I are looking for a mate. But our brothers and sisters are hoping we do."

"Why?"

"They think it will enable Rhoyl to shift back into his male form. If we don't mate, then the dragon can take over."

"So, you're stuck?" Rose asked Rhoyl.

The dragon lifted one-winged shoulder in an approximation of a shrug. He didn't seem concerned that he was stuck.

Rose's gaze shifted to Elek. "And you'll get stuck as a dragon if you don't… mate?"

Elek lifted one of his shoulders in a shrug that also seemed unconcerned. "My beast is under control."

"So… this isn't some kind of trick?" asked Rose. "You're not trying to get in my pants?"

"No." Elek sat more food on her plate. "I wouldn't fit in your pants. You barely fit in your pants. Eat up."

Rose pulled the plate to her. It was another helping of the meat dish, along with another flower. Looking at it, her mouth watered. But her belly protested. She knew that sign. It meant she was full. Only for the first time in her life, she believed it might be true.

"Can I have a doggie bag?" she asked.

Elek frowned.

"It means can you wrap this up so I can save it for later."

"When you want more, I'll make you more. Just ask."

Rose settled back in her chair. Her belly was full. She felt fatigued, but not the normal weariness of her life. She wasn't sure what this full feeling was. But she realized there was one thing missing.

"Where's my sister?"

"She's probably with Ilia."

"Ilia?" Rose's lip curled at that name. "The one who tied us up?"

"The binding is a ritual," said Elek. "We do it

when we think we've found our mate. We bind her so that we can safely introduce the dragon to her, so that he can mark and claim her."

"But, wait." Rose pushed back from the table. "You said I don't have to mate."

"You don't. It's your choice. Ilia has made it known that he wants to claim your sister."

"He what?"

"She has to accept."

"And if she doesn't?"

"Ah…" Elek put the spoon down. "There is the catch you mentioned."

Rose didn't wait for an explanation. She took off out of the kitchens in search of her sister and that beast of a man Ilia. Who knew? He'd probably tied her up again.

CHAPTER NINE

Ilia sat on the couch next to his mate. There was enough distance between them to fit a whole body, maybe even two. But he could still smell Lily's flowery scent. Although it was quickly being masked with the smell of cheese and processed meat.

Lily sat in the very corner of the couch. Her profile was to Ilia as she continually reached over to the side table. On the side table were Ilia's daily snacks, which were dwindling fast under Lily's attention.

In her hands were circular disks of bologna, a square block of neon-orange cheese, which she stacked between ridged crackers like a sandwich. She crunched into the Lunchable in two bites. When she was done, she licked her fingers and began a new stack.

Ilia watched as his snack stash was quickly depleted. Already, Lily had devoured two Twinkies, a cherry Hostess Pudding Pie, and she was eyeing the Cheese Balls near his gaming console. As she was done with the meat, cheese, and crackers of the Lunchable, she now turned her attention to the dessert portion of the meal. With a flick of her painted thumb, she popped open the small box of Nerds and dumped them in her mouth. When she caught him watching, she froze.

Ilia could tell that the hard candies were still on her tongue. She hadn't swallowed them down yet. She stayed still, like one of those life-sized mannequin dolls. He remembered watching a movie called *Mannequin* where a woman was frozen in a substance called plastic. She only came alive when she was alone with her fated mate.

Well, Ilia was alone with the woman he was fated to be with for the rest of his days. She sat lifeless. The flowery scent of her turned dull. At least there wasn't the acrid scent of fear coming off her, which made him glad. Though he wasn't sure he'd be able to tell over the sugary, cheesy, bologna smell.

"So, Lily… we should get to know each other better."

Lily's jaw moved, crunching the Nerds first on the left side of her jowls, then the right. Finally, she swallowed. She cleared her throat, but the only sound she made was a murmur of acquiescence.

Ilia searched for a topic of conversation. He felt like Brian Johnson in *The Breakfast Club*. The nerdy kid who didn't get either hot Claire or basket-case Allison. At the moment, Ilia wasn't even sure how to talk to a girl. It had never been this hard with a fairy. He'd simply crook a finger, and they'd come, to him and for him.

All of which meant he could do this. She was human. And she was his.

"So… what's your favorite movie?"

Lily cleared her throat a couple more times. Her gaze swinging back to the snacks as she answered. "I really didn't get out to the theaters much."

"But you're from Hollywood?"

"LA."

"That's where Arnold Schwarzenegger lives. Did you know him?"

"No."

"Well, I suppose not. He is a big movie star. And he rules California, right?"

"No."

"As the Governor?"

"He was the Governor," she said. "But that was many years ago."

"Right." Ilia rubbed at his chin. "Time moves differently here in the Veil. What year is it over there."

"Over there?" she asked.

"In your part of the world?"

"It's 2020."

"2020? You all made it past 1997?"

"Yes."

"Did you defeat Skynet?"

"Who?"

"That must be it," Ilia said. "If the Terminator was ruling your world, you must have defeated the cyborgs. That's really good news. Though I've always wanted to go up against a T-800. I'm pretty sure I could even take a T-1000; you know, the ones who can shift into liquid."

Lily eyed him warily. She was a skittering thing. But Sarah Connor had been a damsel in the first movie. Ilia had recently watched the second Terminator movie where Sarah Connor became a warrior. He had to admit when Linda Hamilton wielded a gun with those muscular arms and set jaw, it had turned him on.

Looking down at Lily, it was clear she was merely Sarah Connor version one. Ilia worried that he wasn't impressing this damsel even an iota. She seemed more interested in his snacks than she was in his prowess.

She had a handful of Cheeseballs in one palm and was popping one into her mouth with the other. The orange dust landed against her chin like fairy sparkles.

Ilia reached out to brush the flakes away. Before his hand reached her, she jumped back. The orange balls clattered to the floor. Lily looked down with dismay.

"Sorry," he said, gathering the cheesy balls. "I think that's the last batch I have of those. You can't have more for a while because it's gonna cost a high price."

Lily closed her eyes. Her narrow shoulders slumped, and she let out a soul-weary sigh. She looked small and weak and lost.

Ilia didn't want to save her. He wanted to put her to bed. To let her lay all by herself and rest. Lily had not an ounce of fight in her. She looked as though she'd given up.

It was a feeling Ilia wasn't familiar with. Even when he was at his lowest and the odds were against him, there had always been a spark in him. A will to fight.

Lily needed protecting. Not wooing. And she needed more food. He'd have to contact Morrigan about getting in a new shipment of Cheeseballs and Lunchables. He'd likely have to spend a few days in the mine to gather up enough gems in payment. But it would be worth it to give his new family member a spark of happiness.

Hmmm? Family member. Not mate.

Yes. That felt right. Ilia realized that what he felt for Lily, the need to protect and provide was the same he felt for the other girls. His loins didn't ache to get inside her.

Hell, his dragon had been sleeping inside his belly this whole time. The beast hadn't stirred. Not once.

Ilia opened his mouth to suggest he take Lily to get some rest. But the words caught in his throat.

Lily's hands went to her top. She unbuttoned the top button of her shirt. Her fingers trembled as she did so.

"What are you doing?" Ilia asked.

"Getting undressed." Her face was a blank mask as she spoke and worked her clothing.

"Why?"

Lily looked down at his crotch as though it were answer enough. "Isn't this what you want?"

There was no bulge in his crotch. Nothing standing at attention as she continued to undress.

"The other women didn't say it," Lily continued. "They didn't have to. I get it. If I want to stay here, I have to sleep with you. Right?"

Ilia opened his mouth to deny the accusation. Though a few moments ago, she would've been partly right. He had intended to sleep with her and keep her. But he wouldn't have done it against her will.

Looking at her now, he could tell she was acting against her will with no help from him. Lily was passionless about the potential of sleeping with him. Her eyes were vacant. Her movements robotic. She could've been a female model of a T-800.

The door to the game room burst open. A fiery angel stood on the threshold. Her body was tense. Fists clenched. Her toned arms glistened as she raised a fist at him.

Ilia's first thought was that it was Sarah Connor. Not from the first movie. It was vengeful Sara from

T2: Judgement Day. Standing before him was the woman that was a little crazed after what she'd been through in the first film.

"I'm going to kill you," said the avenging angel in the door.

Instead of being wary, Ilia's beast sat up and drooled at the sight of Rose. His cock strained in his pants, eager to get out and at her. Inside him, his dragon roared one single word.

Mine.

ose took one look at her sister lying docile on the couch. Her shirt was unbuttoned. There was a vacant look in Lily's eyes that Rose had seen before. Rose had seen that look the last time her sister had been caught in this kind of position. Only that time, Rose had been too late.

That time Lily had tugged Rose out of the room and brought them home. They had gotten their prescriptions refilled. But even with the medication in their bellies, neither of them had been able to hold down any of the food they'd purchased.

Rose's full belly rioted at seeing Ilia over her sister. It wasn't the same ill feeling she'd gotten after walking in on that casting couch. There wasn't the same nausea gripping her gut. There wasn't the taste of bile coming up her throat.

No. This felt like a burning. Hot and green like when Natasha Sotale got the cover of *Candy Cane* magazine over her. That cow.

But that wasn't Natasha on the couch with Ilia. It was Rose's baby sister. Her twin, whose thigh was within inches Ilia's package.

Rose launched herself at him, hurling her body over the couch. The air was knocked out of her as she made impact. But there was no pain. She was caged in two bars of warm, fleshy muscle.

"Excellent tackle attempt," Ilia said, his hold tightening around her. "Because I'm taller and heavier than you, you should've gone for my knees."

He set her on her feet. Rose wobbled when he let her go. He took a step back from her, squatting into a low fighting stance.

For a moment, Rose stood stunned. Some of the adrenaline leaving her body. She stood as tiny as a David before a massive Goliath, regardless of how he was trying to make himself seem small.

"Are you toying with me?" she asked.

"I'm teaching you," he said. "You got in a good shot earlier when you clocked my nose."

"You mean when you had me tied up?"

"When you're at full strength, I'll show you how to take me down."

"Don't sleep in the meantime," she said. "I don't need my full strength to cut your throat."

His grin was wide, sharp with gleaming teeth. There was a part of her that urged her to flee in the sight of this predator. But another part, a part from somewhere deep inside of her that she wasn't sure she was ever aware, was awakening. That part which came from the vicinity of her long-empty belly was hungering. Something inside her twisted and turned, but not for want of food.

"Rose."

Rose dropped her guard and turned at the sound of her sister's voice. Lily still sat on the couch. The swell of her breast could be seen leaning outside of her blouse.

Rose's mind flashed back to another time when her sister was arranging her clothing after rising from a couch.

"I did it for you," her sister had said back then.

Because that was the only way they'd gotten the job. Getting the job gave them money to get their medication. Getting their medication allowed them to put food in their belly, which gave them the energy to go and get more jobs. The cycle never ended.

Except from that day on, they went into castings together.

Rose had no desire to model. She didn't want to use her body to make money. She'd rather cover up with a burlap sack. But the world only cared about how she looked.

"Rose," said Lily, "it's fine."

"He was about to assault you," said Rose, holding her fists out in front of her. "That is not fine."

"Hey, you're the one who assaulted me," Ilia said to Rose.

The beast of a man loomed over them both, but his attention was fixed on Rose and not Lily. That's when Rose noticed a few things. Ilia's too-small shirt was still on. His pants still rested on his hips and not down around his ankles. She remembered that when he was on the couch, his hands weren't on Lily. Lily's hands had been on him.

"We do not force women," Ilia was saying. "Not anymore. That was the way of our father. Now, if we want a woman to mate with us, we must seduce her into saying yes."

Why did that—the idea of Ilia's seduction— sound like more of a threat than him grabbing her and having his way with her? Perhaps because with seduction, she would let him grab her and then let him have his way with her.

Rose backed up until her sister was within reach. Slowly, Ilia's gaze lifted, tracking her movement. His hand raised to his head, and he scratched at his temple. As he did so, his muscles flexed.

That's when Rose felt that hunger deep inside again. Her knees knocked together. She decided to press her thighs together and was surprised at the relief from the pressure there.

Ilia lifted his nose and inhaled. A wicked smile spread across his face and those sharp teeth made another appearance. "Trust me, I've never taken a female against her will. I'm usually trying to run them off."

"He wasn't raping me," said Lily. "I was going to let him. It's the only way we can stay here. Rose, I want to stay here."

Rose took in more of the room. The empty snack containers on the floor and table. The dusting of orange flakes on Lily's cheek. They wouldn't just be able to survive here. They would thrive.

But this was the catch. And one of them would have to fondle the balls.

"Not you," she said to Lily. Then she turned her

gaze to Ilia. "If sleeping with you is a condition of staying here, then you can have me. Not her."

Ilia scratched at his chin, all the while scrutinizing her face. Not her body. Still, Rose felt the same hollow pit in her stomach as when a casting director was looking her over, seeking her flaws and preparing to proposition or reject her.

"All right," Ilia said.

"All right? You accept me as your mate, or whatever?"

"It's not that simple." There was that toothsome grin again. Though this time, the sharp edges of his incisors glinted in the light of the room. "The rule is, I have to seduce you first."

CHAPTER ELEVEN

*S*he walked with such purpose. Ilia's eyes tracked Rose as she climbed their stairs to the second floor of the castle. Her long-legged stride ate up the distance as she made her way down the hall. The sway of her ass made his incisors sharpen. His claws poked out of his skin. His dragon was clawing at his chest to get out, to get at her.

They had deposited Lily in the kitchen with Elek. The last they'd seen of Lily, she had been looking down lovingly at a fruit pie that Elek had been pulling out of the oven. Lily had barely glanced up at Rose as she gave her assurances that she would be just fine.

Rose stopped her forward motion now. Her feet came together. Her ass cheeks made the shape of an upside-down heart as she stood there. She cleared her throat once, twice. Until finally, Ilia glanced up.

The glare in her eyes told him that he'd been caught staring. He was going to be caught doing a lot more than that.

"Where are we doing this, T-Rex?"

Ilia blinked. "T-Rex? As in Tyrannosaurus Rex?"

She quirked an eyebrow at him, crossing her arms at her chest. The move plumped up her breasts, making her forearms a shelving unit for her tits.

Rose snapped her fingers, bringing Ilia's attention back up to those sparkling eyes of hers.

"I'm not a dinosaur," he said. "They're mostly extinct."

Some of the ire went out of her at that pronouncement. "Mostly?"

"The only living specimens live deep within the core of the earth with the Goddess and her Eloheem. I believe humans call them angels."

"Dinosaurs are real?"

"My brothers and I are the descendants of dinosaurs. Dragons were amongst Her first experiments to craft mankind."

Rose was gaping at him now. Ilia discovered he liked having Rose's full attention on him. It was almost as good as when she was throwing a punch at him. But not as good as when she was throwing her whole body at him.

"This is my room." Ilia pointed to the door across the hall. He crossed the length and pushed the door open.

Rose's formerly long strides were hesitant now. She creeped into Ilia's private sanctuary like a mouse who knew the lion would jump out at any turn. Once inside, she turned slowly, sizing up everything. Ilia wished he had taken a moment to clean up the piles of dirty clothing and put away his action figures. He hadn't expected to be gaining a mate today.

Rose stopped at the foot of his massive bed. She took a deep breath, balling her hands into fists at her sides. She pivoted on her heel and tossed herself back onto the mattress, landing in a puff that made the blankets sigh.

"Just do it," she said, flinging her arms out to the sides and parting her thighs.

Ilia couldn't breathe. He couldn't think. He could barely see past the desire in his eyes.

Inside his chest, the dragon ripped his flesh into ribbons, trying to get out, to get at her.

Mine, it thought.

Mine, it growled.

Mine, it swore.

"What are you waiting for?" Rose huffed. "Are you going to fuck me or what?"

Ilia wanted to groan. He wanted nothing more than to part her thighs and sink himself into her. But when he scented the air, he didn't smell a hint of arousal. The air held the acrid scent of fear.

He stalked slowly toward the bed. As he did so, he pulled tight the reigns on his dragon. He had to. The beast within him was ready to pounce regardless of the sour smell his mate was giving off.

"You're afraid of me?" Ilia said. "Why?"

"Oh, I don't know?" Rose propped herself up on her elbows and glared at him. "Maybe because you kidnapped me. You're holding me against my will. You were about to force yourself on my sister. And now you're going to use me as a sex slave for room and board."

Ilia frowned. "Absolutely none of that is true."

She lunged off the bed and was in his face in an instant. Her index finger pointing at his chest. Ilia barely stopped the instinct to nip that finger.

"Don't lie to me," she demanded.

"I never lie," he said. "I'm not clever enough to

keep all the stories straight. Much easier to stick with the truth since it's what really happened."

Ilia stepped toward her. Close enough that her fingertip pressed against his chest. The moment he made contact with her was a dangerous second. His dragon slipped its leash. Quick as a snake, his tongue struck out and licked at her finger.

Rose gasped. She tried to pull her hand away. But it was too late. The entire digit was inside Ilia's mouth.

He laved at the single digit. Flicking his tongue up and over her nail. Down and around her knuckle. She tasted of salty snacks and sweet treats and something musky that was singularly her.

Ilia knew that musky taste was what waited for him between her thighs. Never again would the honey of a fairy do for him. Only Rose's bitter-sweetness.

With one final lick from his dragon and suckle from Ilia as a man, the two parts of him released Rose's finger. She wobbled as though his lips had been the only thing holding her up. Ilia wrapped a hand around her waist and brought her back against the bedpost. Now when he inhaled, he smelled the pungent aroma of arousal.

"I didn't kidnap you," he began in a low voice. "The Valkyrie saved you. Neither are you being held against your will. You can tell me no and leave at any time."

Rose swallowed but seemed to have trouble. Her throat worked as she took in short breaths. "If that's true, then why did you tie me up?"

Ilia put his nose next to her mouth. He liked the way her hot breaths smelled. He couldn't wait to taste her lips. The ones on her mouth as well as her sex.

"The ropes are part of the ritual," he said, brushing his cheek against hers. "But they're more for your safety than anything."

"My safety?" The two words were said breathlessly.

"When a dragon mates, both man and beast have to agree. Which means the dragon has to meet his female. If she makes any sudden moves, things could get out of hand."

"Meaning the beast in you might force himself on me?"

Ilia pulled away from her. Her lower lip trembled, but he didn't smell that acrid fear anymore. "I would never hurt you, Rose."

Her eyes searched his. Ilia could feel her desire to want to believe him. He knew that feeling so intimately. All the times he'd craved a soothing hand, only to have any kindness slapped away by his father.

It was Ilia's brothers that kept him alive during the worst of it. They would offer him bread, or a bone, or a ratty blanket to keep his small body warm. Much like Rose was trying to do for her sister.

He wanted to wrap his wings around her and never let anything near her. From this day forward, he would be her protector. He would provide everything she needed.

"I'm going to take care of you," he said, brushing a strand of hair past her temple and behind her ear.

Rose shuddered as she looked at him, her gaze hooded. "Are you going to tie me up again?"

Ilia grinned. "I get the feeling you'd like that."

Rose blinked. The second of her lashes touching down against her cheek and fluttering back to meet her brows, her entire countenance changed. "I wouldn't like it at all."

Ilia wasn't one to lie. He truly did find the matter too confusing to bother with. But he was excellent at knowing when someone else was lying. Especially when she smelled of overripe blossoms when she did so.

"I don't like sex," she said.

That smelled true. Ilia straightened and regarded her. "You don't like sex?"

"Of course not. I'm a woman. Sex is for men."

"I don't believe that's the way the Goddess designed it to work."

"Men trade favors for sex," she said.

"I told you, I won't force you." Ilia couldn't abide the doubt on her face. But he also smelled the bittersweet heat coming off her pores. She wanted him. She just wasn't ready to admit it. That was fine by him. They had forever. "In fact, I won't touch you until you beg me to."

"So you won't touch me unless I want you to? Unless I say it?"

Rose broke out into a smile, and Ilia lost his breath.

"Deal," she said.

Ilia took her hand. A trail of heat skittered up his arm. He saw her shiver before she yanked her hand away.

"So, what do you do with a woman if you're not going to fuck her?"

Ilia's face split into a grin. "Loads! Let me show you."

CHAPTER TWELVE

If she heard the woman scream one more time, Rose was going to bang her head against the wall.

On the screen, a scantily-clad, pixilated woman raised a hand to her head. Or at least Rose thought that was a hand. The graphics on this game were too bad to tell for sure.

A dot-grid brute picked up the pixilated princess and ran off with her. The brute could've been an ape or a dragon? The color blocking was all over the place with greens and browns. So Rose couldn't tell.

"See," said Ilia, chucking his head at the screen and not his fingers, which were occupied with the joystick to the video game. "The evil villain has captured the princess. It's now my duty to save her."

The villain dropped the princess up on a high tower, then climbed back down in a blink without moving his arms or legs. Instead of walking down the tower or punching the villain in the nose, the pixilated princess screamed again.

Rose pressed her fingers to her temples. What the game lacked in high definition and a believable plot, it made up for in stereophonics.

"Watch this move," said Ilia. "It's really complicated and took me weeks to learn."

Ilia's fingers flew over the controls. On the screen, Ilia's character, who was a beige-faced man with a mustache, spun and jutted out a leg, making the villain step back. Fire spouted out of the villain's mouth.

So, all those green and brown dots turned out to be a dragon. How apropos. Or rather cannibalistic, given who the hero was controlled by in real life.

Triumphant horns blared as the villain went from upright to flat out on the ground in a blink. The dragon stayed down on the ground, a gray plume of defeat coming out of his mouth. Ilia dropped the controls and thrust his hands into the air.

"I won," he exclaimed. "Didn't you see?"

Rose sat on the farthest end of the couch away

from him. True to his word, he hadn't touched her or tried to make a move. No, instead, he made her sit and watch as he played video games. She had never imagined anything could be any worse than going on a casting call and being objectified.

She was just proven wrong.

"So, you see. I'm not a villain. I just saved the princess."

Rose knew she should humor him. He was a fire-breathing dragon who was holding her captive in real life. But her tongue had always had a mind of its own.

"You do realize the princess could've simply walked down the stairs to find her own freedom?"

Ilia stared at Rose as though he didn't understand what she was saying.

"I mean, that's what I would've done, especially if I was dressed in nothing but a few skimpy rags. Poor girl must be cold."

"She's wearing a beautiful ball gown."

Rose snorted. No woman would dare be caught in that Pepto-Bismol pink concoction. "Why is she even a part of this game? The story clearly has nothing to do with her."

"She has to be saved. She's the hero's very reason for existing."

"No, his reason for existing is to beat the villain. The princess is nothing but an excuse for the dragon and the hero to measure their dicks."

"They don't have dicks in this game."

"Why does she have boobs popping out of her gown? They shouldn't have bothered wasting all those graphics and just made her a round ball that they were fighting over. But I suppose a ball can't scream, and they needed more sound effects."

Ilia stared. His jaw slack. His brows near to his hairline.

"What? You can't really expect a woman to like a game where her entire gender is shown as the weaker sex?"

The look on his face said that was exactly what he thought. Or rather, that he'd never even once thought about it.

"She's put in distress, from which she clearly can escape on her own. She's the hero's motivation for the quest so he can prove his prowess. I'm only surprised she wasn't tied up and tossed onto railroad tracks, and the villain didn't stand by and twirl his mustache."

Ilia's slackened jaw perked up. "What game is that?"

"Look, I've never liked video games. The women

depicted are either a prize, a treasure, or a goal. She's a possession that's stolen, and the men fight over her. At least she should be given the ability to fight for her own freedom."

"You mean so that she can rescue herself?" Ilia asked.

"Yes. That is what modern women do."

"You still think I'm the villain here. You still think you're in need of rescue."

Ilia hunched over, resting his elbows on his knees and his chin in his hands. He looked every bit the little boy whose ball Rose had just deflated.

"I just want a safe place for me and my sister. A place where I can do honest work and not have to watch my back in fear some man will try to throw me on my back and take something he thinks belongs to him."

"I won't throw you on your back, Rose." His features were solemn, as though he was a Boy Scout making her a promise. Then in the blink of an eye, the Boy Scout shifted into a man with sinful thoughts on his mind. "Not unless you ask me to."

Rose felt hot. The same heat she'd felt when Ilia had backed her against his bedpost. She'd expected him to throw her on the bed and take her. When he didn't, it had left her breathless. Not the relieved kind.

"As for a house," he went on, "you can have any room in this castle."

"I thought I was sleeping in your room?" Why did her voice sound so breathless? She didn't want to sleep in his room.

A slow grin spread over his features. His eyes did a lazy tilt down from her head, to her chest, and then her lap, where she had her hands folded primly. Men had ogled her since she was a teen, likely before as well. Their stares had always made Rose feel dirty.

Not this time. Everywhere Ilia's gaze touched, it left a heat trail. How was he doing that? It must be the dragon inside him.

"You're welcome anytime in my room. I'll eagerly await your arrival every night."

"Oh yeah?"

"Yeah."

"Don't hold your breath cause you'll be waiting a long time."

"Did you know dragons can breathe underwater? I can hold my breath for a very..." He leaned in close, then closer, all without touching her. "...very long time."

There was space for her to get up and run. Enough room to reach out and slap him if he did anything wrong. Only none of this felt wrong. Why didn't it feel wrong?

"It's hot in here," she said. "I want to go outside."

"If you want to go out, I'll need to mark you. Otherwise, the lions, bears, and wolves will think you're fair game."

She ignored the lions, bears, and wolves comment and focused on the other thing. "*Mark* me?"

"I would have to bite you, which would leave a mark. So that the others would know you're mine, and no one would touch you."

"*Bite* me?"

He nodded. "At the base of your neck, so everyone will see."

His gaze latched onto Rose's neck. The spot where her shoulder met her neck column burned. That burn radiated heat throughout her chest, making her nipples hard.

Ilia cocked his head to the side like he could see the temperature inside her rising. The tingling sensation increased. Rose knew her cheeks, her chest, both had to be red.

He made no mention of it. He simply glanced at

her, his tongue snaking out of his mouth to lick at his lower lip. But he didn't pounce. He didn't reach for her.

The realization that he wouldn't, that he truly would do nothing unless she asked him to, left Rose with a surge of power running alongside that heat.

"Will it hurt?" she asked.

"No. I would never do anything to cause you pain or sorrow."

"Fine."

"Fine… what?"

He was going to make her say it. "Bite me."

She hoped her tone conveyed the opposite meaning of that phrase that had been popularized in the eighties. Ilia, being a connoisseur of that long-ago time period, smirked as though he caught her drift. Instead of taking offense, he threw back his head and laughed.

When his gaze came back to her, Rose saw the predator behind his gem-colored eyes. She should run. She wasn't trapped. She could make it to the door.

Rose held still and waited.

CHAPTER THIRTEEN

Ilia let the joystick slip from his grip. He was no longer interested in holding the plastic controller. Not when he'd just been offered the opportunity to handle a warm, supple woman.

He'd told her he wouldn't touch her without her permission. That didn't mean he wouldn't look. And look his fill, he did.

Rose was aroused. Her pink lips were flushed, just like a flower whose bud was ready to burst open. With each of her quick breaths, her breasts rose higher, straining the top of her blouse. Even if he couldn't see it with his own eyes, he scented that she was aroused.

She wanted him. She just couldn't bring herself

to admit it. Which was why in the past, dragons often tied up the women brought to serve their needs.

For a long time, women had been taught to be shameful of their desires. But if they were tied down, then they would have no responsibility in assuaging their needs. The ropes would set them free.

Except Ilia didn't have any rope in the game room. He didn't want to leave Rose while the heat of want was coursing through her blood. Her pupils were dilated. Her lips parted with sweet, shallow breaths escaping.

She'd breathed the same way when he'd tied her up the first time. Her entire body had gone languid from the pull of the ropes. His groin tightened with the memory.

There had to be something in this room he could use?

The chip-tune sounds of the game played on in the silence between Ilia and Rose. The descending bass notes let Ilia know that his character had lost, and the villain had won. For the first time in his gaming life, Ilia understood why the villain desired to kidnap the damsel and fight to the death to keep her.

This damsel was not going to get away from Ilia. Pretty soon, she would be cheering to have him wrap his arms around her. Hopefully, after his bite, Rose would want more than just his teeth sunk inside her.

"Give me your hands," he said.

Rose's lashes fluttered. The haze lifted, and her gaze narrowed as Ilia reached down to the floor. He grabbed the controller and pulled until the console slid across the floor to him. Once he had the box in hand, he tugged out the cords and cables.

The sound of the music cut off.

The screen went blank.

"Hands," he repeated.

"Why?" she demanded.

Unlike any of the times she'd spoken to him earlier, there was no bite to her tone. She sounded breathy, as though she was trying to swallow down her desire. But couldn't.

"You're not going to tie me up again?" she said. "Are you?"

"Yes." Ilia stretched the length of one of the cables. It was twice the length of his arm. Perfect.

"I said I'd let you bite me, or whatever." Rose's gaze was on the cable.

"I'm going to bite you." Ilia let the cable glide

through his fingers. He stopped when he found the middle. With his index finger and thumb, he pinched the middle section of the cable and let the two ends fall to the sides. "This is part of the ritual."

Rose eyed the length. Her gaze tracked the swinging ends. "You said you wouldn't force me."

She didn't scramble off the couch. She didn't cover her arms over her body to shield herself. She simply watched the sway of the rope.

"Give me your hands." Ilia said the words gently, quietly. Not a hint of force in his voice or in his posture.

Rose's gaze flicked to his. Only briefly. Slowly, she raised her wrists to him.

"You're not my captive," he said. "I am yours."

Ilia wrapped the cable around her torso. His knuckles skated just under her breast. Rose's lids fluttered, but she did not close her eyes. Her gaze stayed focused on his hands.

Just under her breasts, he made a loop. With a flick of his wrist, he pulled the binds, increasing the tension. A small gasp escaped her lips.

"You can get away from me anytime, Rose. I haven't kidnapped you. I do have every intention of keeping you."

Ilia wrapped the cable just above her breast bone.

He made another loop, folding the cable over and under. The end result looked like a flowering rose.

Her arms were bound to her body, leaving her neck and collarbone exposed for Ilia's mark. The dragon inside him clawed at his belly, ripping it to shreds to be let out. To be let at her. But Ilia wasn't done with his conversation.

"I want to go on an adventure together with you. We must first pass this level."

"Because when you mark me, it'll give me special powers?"

He grinned. "Exactly. Everyone in our world will know you're protected and that they'll have me to contend with if they dare mess with you."

Ilia tugged the rope tight. The tightness was for her protection. His dragon wanted her. Any wrong move, and it would pounce. He needed complete control.

"Ready?" he asked.

Rose opened her mouth. Her lips moved. But no sound came out.

Ilia doubted he would've heard her if she made a peep. He likely wouldn't have heard her scream either. The desire rushing through him was too loud.

He tilted her head and struck her neck. The taste

of the salty sweetness of her pulled him under. He was marking her as his own, but when her flesh met his lips, it was clear who had claimed whom.

CHAPTER FOURTEEN

It had to be the food. That's what was making her act so wanton. Like a glutton.

Rose had never been full a day in her life. And now that her belly was full of all the delicious, exotic food, her loins had decided they wanted in on the action.

Well, screw that.

She might have opened her mouth, but the hell if she was opening her legs. Been there. Done that. Didn't want the t-shirt to remember.

What she did remember was that sex had been a messy, awkward, painful affair. She'd only done it once. Everyone said the first time often hurt. But there was the bump your knee ouchie that lasted for a few seconds, and then there was the stub your pinky toe tearing pain that radiated through your entire body and lasted for hours -maybe all day.

Sex with Curt Melber had been a mix of the two. He'd bumped into her untried vagina and continually stubbed her sensitive flesh. Luckily, it had only lasted a few seconds. Which had been long enough.

After that brief encounter, Curt spent the next year telling every male casting director, photographer, and model that he'd *hit that*. From that moment on, Rose had to doubly watch her back—and her front—with men thinking they could tap that ass. Even though they all thought they could tap her ass before her ill-fated virginity loss. With her ass normally being on display on magazine spreads and catwalks, most people thought they had a right to a piece of it.

The second Rose felt Ilia's breath on her neck, her knees unknotted. A small piece of her decided it wanted to be tapped. That piece grew larger and larger, making her wonder if she'd taken a hit of something.

Her hands were bound tight, leaving no room to reach out and push him away. Not that she had a single inclination to do so. Her fingers trembled. Not with fear. With the need to...need for...?

She wasn't sure what she needed. She only knew that she did. She *needed*.

It must be a drug.

Most reptiles had venom in their fangs. He was a dragon. That had to be what was happening. Except? Had he broken the skin?

He must have. It was the only explanation. It was the only reason she wanted to pull him close. But she couldn't. Her hands were bound.

Rose gasped as she felt his teeth on her neck. The twin sharp pinpoints raised over her skin. The bliss of it knocked her knees open wider. The need grew stronger.

What was this heat she was feeling?

What was this ache?

It couldn't be desire? Ilia was a man. With a penis. If she kept acting like this, if her knees kept parting, he was going to want to put that penis inside of her. Then there would be more pain.

Except, she wasn't feeling a single twinge of discomfort. Instead, she wanted—no, she needed more.

Her fingers straightened, needing to reach out and touch Ilia's flesh. To push him away? To bring him closer? She still wasn't sure?

No matter what she wanted, the ropes prevented

her movement. She could get up and run. However, the ropes prevented that too.

Not physically. Her legs were in working order, as proven by her ever more wantonly opening knees. Just like when she'd hung from the ropes in the cave, Rose didn't want to move. She wanted nothing more than to allow the ropes to take all of her weight, all of her worries, all of her cares.

Ilia wasn't touching her, save for the sharp points of his teeth. His body hovered over her form as his teeth sank downward.

Had she missed the pain? He'd said there wouldn't be pain. She hadn't believed that. He was biting her. As his teeth pierced her skin millimeter by millimeter, the need inside her increased until she whimpered.

Ilia licked at the flesh caged between his teeth. She felt the hot wetness spread across her shoulders. Rose was certain he was licking down her spine, drenching each vertebra with fire. That had to be his tongue behind her knee, leaving a trail of damp heat. It was him bathing her inner thighs with a curling steam that made her knees slide wider apart.

When she opened her eyes, she saw the curls of his hair. She saw the profile of his angular face cradled against her neck. She felt his chest heave out a long sigh. Then his cheeks hollowed out, and he pulled.

Rose cried out as his mouth worked on the spot where he'd bitten her. The points of his teeth and the velvety smoothness of his tongue wreaked havoc on her senses. She felt she no longer had control over her limbs.

Her knees were splayed wide, now cradling his torso. She had the urge to lift her legs and wrap them around Ilia, to bring him closer, closer to that need that still plagued her.

She didn't want him inside her. She just wanted him against her to relieve some of that oppressive need that was threatening to consume her. If she didn't get relief soon, she was going to start crying. And she couldn't have that.

"No, please," she sighed.

She wasn't sure what she was asking for. Ilia didn't ask for clarification. He shifted his large body and settled a knee between her thighs. Then he went back to licking and suckling at her collarbone.

Rose lay back in unbelievable bliss. Ilia's knee was exactly what she needed. It was exactly where she needed it.

She couldn't move her head with Ilia clamped down against her neck. She couldn't move her upper body as it was bound tight with ropes. The only choice she had left was to move her hips.

She raised her ass and hit the jackpot. The smooth muscles of Ilia's thigh were just what the doctor ordered. The feel of his flesh against hers, even through their two layers of clothing, soothed that need inside her.

The descent of her sex as it came back down to the couch was just as good. No, it was even better. It didn't quite quiet the need inside her. But it certainly pacified it.

Rose lifted her hips again. There, against Ilia's thigh, she found even more comfort, more calm. The sensation was like floating on a cloud. Rose wanted to go higher.

She moved against Ilia. Making her strokes longer, harder, faster.

Up and up, she rose. Flying higher with each stroke. The need never dissipated. It grew bigger, fuller.

Rose's movements became jerky, disjointed, frantic as the need got away from her again. She chased it but feared she wouldn't catch it. Until it turned around and caught her.

By now, the need had grown so big that one

more stroke, one tiny movement, and it would burst.

"No, wait," Rose pleaded.

She wasn't sure if he heard her. She stopped moving. She held perfectly still, afraid of the monster she'd created.

If she kept moving wantonly against, he'd think she… well, wanted it. She couldn't have him think that. Neither could she stop moving. Because she… well, wanted it.

Above her, Ilia gave another pull of his mouth. With that single pull, her need burst.

Rose felt as though her body was flung to the ground. Instead of pain, the impact brought intense pleasure. A pleasure so deep, so all-consuming, that Rose worried she might drown in it.

It would be a good death. Only she didn't want to die. She wanted to do it again.

But that couldn't be right. Could it?

"Yes, no?" She wasn't sure.

The dueling emotions were tugging her apart as the pleasure abated. When she finally managed to open her eyes, she joyed to find that she was still alive. Which meant that she could do it again. But Ilia was pulling away from her.

"No," she protested, reaching for him. Her nails

dug into his chest, breaking the skin it came into contact with.

Ilia's eyes were dark and bright at the same time. The contrast confused her.

"I won't lose control." His words were a rasp as he spoke. Nothing like the carefree man who'd played a kid's video game.

It wasn't his voice. He sounded like a wild creature. He looked like a wild creature. Looking at him closely, Rose saw something lurking beneath the surface of his fine features.

"You need to leave," he said.

With a swipe of his claw, he cut the cables binding her. Rose shivered at the impact of her freedom. Her arms flailed as she tried to remember how to use them.

"Leave, Rose."

She couldn't get her legs to move. She couldn't even brace herself with her hands to rise from the couch. She couldn't remember how. She didn't want to. She wanted the rope back. To tie her down. To alleviate the need to make a decision. To take away some of her choices so that she could focus on what she truly wanted.

What she wanted was stepping away from her.

Ilia's eyes glowed brightly as he looked down at

her. His skin shimmered from the deep tan flesh of a man to the dark scales of a beast.

He was no longer a man. He was all dragon. His wings spanned out to touch both sides of the room. His claws scraped against the floor as he stood to his full height. And that dark purple, near black, gaze tracked her movements.

Not that she had moved from the couch. She still couldn't get her limbs to cooperate in their newfound freedom. What did move through her was fear.

The dragon's nostrils flared. Its features crumpled into something that looked like shame. It backed up toward the windows, claws scraping against the floor with each step.

A thundering crash. The splinter of glass. And it was gone. Out the window and into the night.

Rose's legs and arms finally agreed to coordinate. She stood on shaky limbs. Her fingers went to her neck. She searched until she found the raised skin Ilia had left there. The spot was warm and throbbing, just like the rest of her.

CHAPTER FIFTEEN

"For a strong, purple dragon, you look blue, Ilia. I'm sure Clove and I can brighten your night."

"No, thank you, Honeysuckle."

Ilia hunched over his drink at God's Teet. His back muscles hurt from pushing his wings hard during flight. He'd flown the length of the Veil and back to keep his dragon from Rose.

"I'm sure you don't mean that," said Honeysuckle in her tinkling voice. She laced her viney fingers around Ilia's bicep.

"No, means no." Ilia plucked the fairy's fingers from his arm and turned back to his drink.

"No, it doesn't," said Clove. "Not when you're a beast."

"Definitely not when you're a beast of a dragon," said Honey.

"Beasts need sex," said Clove. "Which is why the Goddess made fairies. So dragons, and bears, and wolves, and lions and fairies could fuck without the consequence of sucklings."

"It's the perfect relationship," agreed Honey. "Now, let's go out in the field and pollinate some night flowers."

"I said no." Ilia enunciated each word. He was dangerously close to popping the head off these overgrown plants. Lucky for them, he would never hurt a female.

Unless she was his mate.

"It has to be a human," Clove was saying as she backed away from Ilia.

"I'm sick of these warmbloods coming in and taking our fuck buddies," Honey agreed.

Their voices faded into the background as thoughts of Rose bloomed inside Ilia's mind. Ilia had failed. He hadn't even passed the first level of seduction with his mate before he'd gone up in flames. She'd told him no. She'd said the word more than once. Yet, in his desire for her, he hadn't heard her.

Or worse, he had heard her. He'd simply ignored her plea.

He picked up the goblet of flames and tossed it back. The burn down his throat felt like a penance. The problem was, he wanted to commit the sin again. And then again.

Just the thought of Rose's flesh in his mouth. The taste of her life's blood on his tongue. The scent of her honeyed arousal in his nose.

That she'd been aroused even as she rejected him was still a point of confusion for Ilia. But he couldn't mistake that single-syllabled word. Nor could he discount the evidence of her attempt to push him away from her.

Any other night, he'd have worn Rose's scratches on his flesh like a badge of honor. Tonight, they were his shame. From inside his chest, he could feel his dragon licking at the wounds her nails had made as she'd tried to push him away.

Ilia wasn't fooled by the beast's placations. His dragon wanted to get out. It wanted to fly back to the castle. To throw its mate down and claim her in the ancient ways of its kind.

Hard. Rough. Rutting.

That was what the beast inside him wanted. The beast below in his pants, as well. If Ilia was honest with himself, it was what he wanted with every bone in his body, including his boner.

But Rose had said no. At least he had enough presence of mind to get out of the room before his dragon or his dick took over and claimed her against her will.

"Another one." Ilia held up his empty mug.

Mari raised a dubious brow as she refilled his mug and lit the flame. "I see you came to your senses and didn't go beyond the Veil."

"Didn't need to," Ilia said after taking a sip. "Morrigan brought back two females."

"Two?" Mari's second brow lifted to join the first. "You're going to mate two women? I always took you for a glutton, but this is beyond the pale."

"They're not both for me. Just Rose. Though she'll never trust me again." Ilia held out his empty mug for yet another refill. "She told me no, and I didn't listen."

Mari took the mug and poured. "So the other human is for Elek?"

"Who? Lily? No, I had originally chosen Lily. But after getting to know Rose, I knew she was the one for me. Rose has the fire of Sarah Connor in her, but she's a little cray-cray like Allison Reynolds from *The Breakfast Club*. You know, the dark-haired one."

"Right, right." Mari struck the match for the

brew, but it didn't take the first time. "And Lily's mating Elek?"

"Elek doesn't want a mate," Ilia said, taking the match from Mari and lighting his drink himself. "But now Rose thinks I'm a villain because she told me no, and I didn't listen."

"Because Rose wants Elek?"

"Rose is mine."

The top of the brew burst into flames. The fire didn't stop there. It spread across the counter, aiming for the store of alcohol.

Marigold stretched out her arm. With a flick of her wrist, the fire stopped in its tracks. With the curl of her fingers, ice covered the flames. The mix turned into a puddle of water on the bar.

"Sorry, Mari."

"It's fine," Mari said as she used a rag to wipe up the spilled brew. "You're understandably upset about *your* mate, *Rose*."

Ilia liked that Mari clearly and concisely enunciated that Rose was his. He found that he wasn't thirsty anymore. Not for the brew. The only thing he wanted in his mouth was Rose.

"You said Elek won't mate?" Mari wrung the damp rag to within an inch of its life. The last drop of water was anemic as it splattered to the ground without a sound. "So she's for the lions? Or the bears? Or the wolves?"

"Lily's for Rhoyl."

The dried rag slipped from Marigold's hand. It clattered to the ground, also not making a sound. "Rhoyl? He's back in male form?"

"No. Hopefully, having a mate will coax him to finally shift back. Mari? Are you okay? You look as though you smell something foul."

"I'm—" Mari cleared her throat. When her gaze met Ilia's again, she was back to her no-nonsense self. "I'm fine. Tell me what you did to upset your mate?"

"I marked her."

"And?"

"I lost control."

"And?"

"I wanted to throw her down and rut on her."

"I realize I'm sounding like a broken record here, Ilia. But... and?"

"She was writhing against me, taking her pleasure. And then she said no."

Mari cocked her head to the side. "How did she say no?"

"What do you mean how? When a woman says no, she means no."

He glanced up at Mari. But the fairy's face was an impassive mask once more. Though he sat, Ilia shuffled his feet against the sticky floor. His dragon wanted to go, but the man wasn't certain of his direction.

"She thinks I'm the villain of our game," Ilia said.

"Game?" said Mari. "Don't you mean love story?"

"That's what I said."

"Technically, she's right," said Mari. "She was kidnapped."

"By Morrigan."

"Then you took her to a high castle full of guarded treasure."

"That's where I live," said Ilia.

"It's what villains do. Heroes are the ones that come to the rescue."

Ilia's cheeks burned. That fire came from within, not the drink that sat untouched in front of him. Mari was right. He hadn't rescued Rose. He'd taken her from captivity and placed her in a gilded cage.

"Then you forced yourself on her?" Mari continued.

"No." But his denial was wobbly. "I said I wouldn't mark her unless she asked me to. She said yes… at first. And then she said no."

Though now that he thought of it, she had said *please* and *no*. She had said *wait* and *no*. *Yes* and *no*.

She had said no, all while moaning her desire. She had moaned her desire while writhing her lower body against his thigh. She had cried out a denial as her orgasm had taken her.

Did her no actually mean no?

Inside of his chest, his dragon gave him a mighty kick. His dragon would've never hurt its mate. It would lay down its very life for her.

Could that be the reason both Ilia and his beast had ignored Rose's pleas? Because she hadn't meant what he thought she meant? Maybe she hadn't even meant what she thought she meant?

CHAPTER SIXTEEN

Rose really wasn't in the mood for dinner. Didn't they just have dinner? Everyone in this castle seemed to be eating all the time.

Be it a full course meal. Or snacks left out around television sets, gaming consoles, and near fireplaces. If not putting food directly into their mouths, then they were putting their tongues down each other's throats.

Cardi used a finger to gloss her lips with wine. Then she smiled up at Kimber, who diligently sipped the beverage from her lips.

Poppy sat on Beryl's lap as she fed him bits of what looked like flowers. He'd take a bite of the greens and then nip the side of her mouth.

And then there was Corun and Chryssie. The father to be cut up his mate's food into tiny bites. He stabbed morsels onto his fork in the same pattern, delivering them to her waiting mouth. All while Chryssie gazed adoringly at him.

For the first time since she'd been here, Rose felt sick to her stomach. Despite the savory aroma of the dish in front of her, her appetite was nowhere to be found. She didn't want to eat, but neither did she want to be alone.

Unfortunately, she couldn't sneak off with her sister. Lily was entranced by every plate Elek brought to the table. She listened intently as he described the ingredients and how he'd prepared each item. Rose wasn't even sure her sister knew she was in the room, as she was so engrossed with the food and the chef.

Looking around the room, she didn't see Ilia. Which was fine. It didn't bother her. Not one bit. She didn't care if she didn't see him again.

A whoosh sounded at the large window on the opposite side of the dining room. The window took up nearly the entire wall. A set of claws tugged open the pane, and the body of a large dragon fit itself inside. The dragon was of the deepest blue, not of a jaded purple.

It wasn't Ilia.

Rose huffed out a breath. She slumped back in her chair and crossed her arms over her chest. When her forearms brushed against her breasts, she noted her nipples were hard as rocks. Which was unusual as it wasn't cold in the dining room, and she wasn't in a bathing suit.

Because swimwear spreads were often shot in the winter, models had to contend with headlights blaring into the camera. Right now she wore too many layers to give anyone a show. No one was paying attention to her to notice.

Definitely not the man who had made her nipples that hard to begin with. He wasn't even around to see what he was doing to her. He'd just up and flew away.

"Does your belly ache, Rose?" asked Elek, his gaze attentive. "Do you possess an aversion?"

"Aversion?" asked Rose.

"He means an allergy," said Cardi. "To the food. Is it upsetting your stomach?"

That would make a great excuse for Rose's discomfort. But she felt no aches or pains. There was a hollowness in her chest and an ache between her thighs. Would food cure that?

Rose dug into the dish. It wasn't like she had to

model anymore. At the first bite, her tastebuds screamed for more. It was delicious. But it wasn't satisfying. She wanted something with a bit more spicy fire and salty sweat.

Elek smiled at her with a kind, non-predatory expression on his face. Lily smiled at Elek as though the dragon shifter were made of chocolate—something that was overflowing on Lily's plate.

Food was overflowing on every woman's plate. If the figures of the other women were anything to go by, the dragons seemed to like a lot of flesh on their women's bones. Chryssie, Cardi, and Poppy weren't thin waifs. They all had curves.

"More?" Elek asked, holding out a large serving spoon filled with more of the delicious fare.

Rose's belly was full. That other ache lower down in her body remained persistent. "Maybe we should leave some for Ilia."

"We won't run out of food," said Corun. "There'll be plenty left for Ilia when he joins us. Where is he? In the mines?"

Rose didn't answer, as she didn't know where he'd flown off to after leaving her shivering and trembling from his touch. Instinctively, Rose lifted her hand to her neck and touched the still throbbing twin pinpricks Ilia had left there.

"I'm surprised he's not here with you, Lily," said Kimber. "After a dragon marks his mate, he's loathe to leave his female."

"Ilia didn't mark Lily," said Elek, his gaze fastened on Rose's neck.

The room went silent as all gazes fell to Rose. Each woman's mouth spread into a stupid grin as they snuck less-than-covert gazes at Rose. The males' brows all rose to their hairlines as they stared at the spot on her neck. Rose was used to people staring at her, but she felt uncomfortable at the gaping expressions on their faces.

Kimber was the first to speak. "Thank you for choosing my brother, Rose."

She hadn't chosen him. She'd merely shoved her sister out of harm's way. Still, the thought of Lily receiving Ilia's bite, of her sister rubbing her sex against Ilia's thigh…

"Ilia was born the runt of the litter, you know," Kimber said in a conversational tone.

"What does that mean?" Rose asked.

"Dragons are born in pairs."

"Like us?" It was the first time Lily had spoken. There had been food in her mouth since Rose entered the dining room. There was food in Lily's mouth now as she spoke. She shoveled more forkfuls in to Elek's delight.

"Yes, like twins," said Kimber. "But Ilia was a third. He was born small and undernourished. Our father decided Ilia wouldn't make it. So he tossed him outside shortly after his birth."

Lily stopped eating. Her utensil clattered to the plate. Both she and Rose mimicked each other like when they had trouble swallowing the food in their mouths.

Rose had thought she had it bad, but at least her father put a roof over their heads while he'd lived. He'd had to. His exotic-looking daughters had been his bread and butter.

"Ilia has had to fight for every scrape," Kimber continued. "Now that you're here and mated to him, I hope his fighting days are over."

Another whoosh sounded above them. Rose looked up to the window to see a massive dragon. Its dark purple scales blended with the night's sky. Its bright gaze fixed on her.

Rose's full belly grumbled loudly. The dish in front of her went forgotten as she saw the dessert she craved begin to shift its form from beast to man.

CHAPTER SEVENTEEN

Ilia slammed the bedroom door shut behind Rose. The fact that she didn't jump out of her skin let him know that she didn't fear him. Another thing he'd gotten wrong from their time together earlier.

She hadn't argued with him as he told her to come with him. She'd simply put down her fork and knife. Then she'd risen from her chair and followed him to his room.

Now that they were inside, her sharp intake of breath added further proof that she wasn't afraid to be alone with him. In fact, he was becoming more certain with each passing second that she had less of a problem being alone with him than he had of being alone with her.

Inside his chest, Ilia's beast was pacing. His dragon looked out from behind Ilia's gaze, tracking her every movement. It was waiting for its opportunity to pounce. The animal inside the man got the sense that his moment was coming nearer as its mate's gaze roamed over his naked form.

Rose's nostrils flared as her light eyes latched onto the dark hair surrounding his engorged cock. Ilia hadn't bothered to don any clothing when he'd shifted from dragon to man. His brothers didn't care. His sisters were so used to it that they ignored him—though he was sure he'd caught Cardi sneaking a glance once or twice. Lily had dropped her fork when she'd seen him in all his glory.

But Rose? His Rose had wet her lips. Her fingers had curled into balls atop the dinner table. Ilia had caught those motions in the split second before she averted her gaze.

She wanted him. So why was she denying it? He was about to find out.

"I've made a decision, Rose."

"What? That you won't run out on me again?"

"That was a mistake, and I apologize for it. But you'll have to admit that my actions were partly your fault."

Her eyes flashed at him. "Me? What did I do?"

"You didn't tell me the truth." Ilia took two steps toward her.

"You're calling me a liar?" Rose took one step back.

"I am." He stepped forward again, crowding her toward the bed. "The worse kind of liar. You lie to yourself."

"I have no idea what you're talking about." Rose's back bumped into the bedpost. Her fingers curled around the wooden pillar.

"You want me."

"I…" Her lips remained parted, but the words wouldn't come out.

In the silence that followed, Ilia realized she was right on one count. He had run out on her. And for that, he was ashamed.

Unlike his father, Rose hadn't tossed him out. She'd let him in, let him get close enough to try to bind himself to her. Because Ilia still had the scars of neglect and abuse, he needed her to open herself up fully. He needed her to welcome him inside whole-heartedly.

His mate stood before him. Her back against a bedpost where she'd soon be writhing on the bed in more pleasure than any woman would ever know. Her tiny pants of breath hinted that she knew what lay in her future.

So why was there struggle in her gaze? The bright glint of her eyes said yes. But the set of her jaw wouldn't let the word out.

"I want to be your champion, Rose Bishop."

That notion set her jaw in motion. "I don't need to be saved."

"Yes. Yes, you do. First, you need to be tied up and held captive. You need someone to capture you. It's the only way you'll be set free."

There was a crinkle at the corner of her eyes. Rose pursed her lips together, clearly uncertain as to what to think of that.

Ilia was done talking. He was standing before his fated mate. Naked, with a raging hard-on and a beast raring to go.

"I'm going to claim you, Rose."

"What does that mean?"

"I'm going to strip you naked, toss you on the bed, and thrust so deeply inside you that you're going to see stars."

The room filled with the heady scent of her arousal. Inside him, the dragon roared to get out. Ilia ground his feet into the floor, battling the beast and his own desire. Before he could let loose, he needed to get his mate's consent.

"Do you want me to do that?" he asked. "Do you want me to make you see stars, sweet Rose?"

"Do I have a choice?" Her lips trembled as her nostrils flared.

"Yes, you have a choice. You always have a choice. Tell me you want me."

Rose swallowed, her throat working as though there was something lodged in there. Her lips did not part to let it out.

"All you have to do is say yes."

She inhaled through her nose, nostrils flaring even wider. That same breath of air gushed back out of her nose. Still, she would not open her mouth.

"Say it, Rose."

Her gaze was wild. As though she were caged inside of herself. Yet, she couldn't break free.

She had fought him when she'd thought he was going to hurt her or her sister. Now that he was offering her pleasure, she couldn't even lift a finger to reach for the bliss.

"Rose?" Ilia held out his hand to her.

Her fingers straightened toward the floor, but she didn't lift her arms. Her feet shuffled, but she didn't raise her heels from the ground.

She wanted him. He could sense it. He could see

it. She just couldn't say it. So, Ilia reached for her blouse and tore.

"Hey!" she said.

"Tell me no," he said, changing tactics. "And I'll stop."

Once again, Rose swallowed like a new lump had formed in her throat. She couldn't say she wanted it. Neither could she deny that she did.

He grabbed the collar of her shirt and tugged down until her arms were trapped in the sleeves. She took a step then. The step was toward him.

Rose's eyes rolled to the back of her head, and her lips parted. She didn't say yes. She didn't say no. She let out a low moan that sounded of pure ecstasy.

"As your mate, I'm supposed to be gentle and make love to you. But I don't think that's what you need right now. I think you need to be fucked."

Though Ilia said the words out loud, in truth, he wasn't sure it was what she needed. It was definitely what he needed. To bury himself so deeply inside this woman that not even the breath of air could get between their groin areas.

"If you don't want this, if you want me to stop, then you'll say Vernon."

"What?" Rose blinked, some of the haze of desire lifting from her.

"That was the name of the principal in *The Breakfast Club*. He's the villain of the film. Nobody liked him. You say Vernon, and I'll stop immediately, no matter how deeply my dick or my tongue is buried inside you."

Rose's throat worked again. This time she had no trouble swallowing the desire in there. Her lips stayed parted, her pupils dilated. The heavy scent of her arousal perfumed the air of his bedroom.

"I think you want me to lick you with my tongue, don't you, sweet Rose?"

"No," she said on a shuddered breath.

"That's not Vernon."

Ilia took a nipple in his mouth. Rose's knees wobbled under the onslaught. Her arms were bound in her shirt, so she couldn't catch herself. She didn't need to. Ilia held her captive.

"You want to be naked in front of me, don't you?"

"No, I don't. You're making me."

So that's how she needed to play it. Fine by him. He would make her. Just so long as he had her consent. And until she cried Vernon, Ilia knew he had her.

With a roar, he ripped the rest of her clothing from her. Save the shirt binding her arms. She stood naked, shivering in his arms.

"I don't know where to start," he said as he took in what was his. "Your mouth, your tits, or your pussy?"

Rose whimpered at his words. Her cries going a higher pitch as he called out each lush body part. Her moan was the highest when he spoke of her pussy, so that's where he decided to start.

"I think you want me to start with this sweet little pussy, don't you, Rose?"

She opened her mouth, but no sound came out. She shook her head instead. With that denial, Ilia lifted her and tossed her on the bed.

Rose yelped as she bounced backward. With her arms tangled in the blouse, her thighs spread in an effort to gain balance. For a moment, she left them open. When she looked up and caught Ilia staring, she shoved them closed.

"Stop," he commanded. "Open for me."

She hesitated. The denial game she could play. When it came to a direct command, she had trouble. Not a problem. He'd simply have to take the decision away from her.

Ilia reached out and grabbed her right leg in one hand. He grabbed the bottom of her shirttails in the other. With a rip of the fabric, he took the strip and tied her ankle to the bedpost. With another strip, he tied the other ankle. Her arms were behind her, still tangled in the sleeves of the garment. The bottom half of her was splayed open for his enjoyment.

"I don't hear you saying no. I think you want this."

"I don't have a choice," she said, her voice barely above a whisper. "You're making me do it."

Ilia parted her thighs. She glistened there. She could say no all she wanted, but her body wanted him. "You want me to suck you so hard I turn this pink pussy red, don't you?"

"No," she pleaded, as her folds dripped and quivered from just the suggestion.

She fell back on the bed, her chest arching upward, tight nipples pointed to the ceiling. She was absolute perfection, and she was all his.

Ilia sank to his knees at the base of the bed. Her spread thighs were an altar, her bent knees like pillars of a temple of worship. He bent over her, prepared to give his devout worship.

"Rose?"

She opened an eyelid.

"You're mine."

Again her throat worked. No lump formed. Her lips parted, but they trembled as they did so.

Ilia waited in the silence of both of their heavy

breaths. He waited as her gaze locked onto his, pleading. He would give this woman anything except this one thing.

"I need you to say it."

She swallowed again. This time her teeth unclenched as she let sound through. "I…"

Ilia brushed his thumb over the bud of her sex. Her head fell back as she jackknifed off the mattress. She couldn't get too far with her feet and hands bound.

"Say it, just once, Rose."

"I…" Her eyes glistened with tears as she struggled. Her arms and feet stayed put. The struggle was all internal.

The sight of his mate's tears overran Ilia's own need for acceptance. He crawled up the bed, placing his big body between her open thighs.

"It's all right," he said as he kissed each tear away. "You belong to me. If you deny it, tell me your safe word."

Rose inhaled a long, slow breath. Her voice was shaky as she let out the single word. "No."

Ilia grinned. That wasn't the safe word. They both knew it.

"You are mine, sweet Rose."

There was only the barest dip of her head, but he

caught it. It was enough. For the time being. Now he had to make good on all the promises of pleasure he'd threatened her with.

CHAPTER EIGHTEEN

Rose felt as though she was being torn apart. Her body was aching for Ilia, but her mind couldn't wrap around the idea of verbally agreeing to anything he was demanding of her.

Having sex with him—opening her thighs and getting thoroughly, deeply, completely fucked—this was what she had to do. It wasn't what she wanted to do.

Right?

Except, as he kissed the tears burning her eyes away, she found herself burning with the need for him to kiss her lips. As his hands cradled her face, she needed his fingers to cup her breasts. As he rested his large body between her thighs, she needed him to enter her quivering pussy and put an end to the ache inside her.

She wasn't supposed to feel this way. Sex was for men, not women. Any female who said differently was lying and using her body to get ahead.

But Ilia had fulfilled her every need. She and her sister had a roof over their head, which he promised would never be taken from them. They no longer needed money because he swore he'd give her anything she wanted. She no longer needed her medication because she was in a place where she could fill her belly without consequence. Moreover, the food was aplenty.

There wasn't a thing she needed in the world. Except for Ilia's hands over her, his mouth on her, and his cock in her. To get that need filled, he asked the impossible of her.

For the countless time tonight, Rose set her mouth to acquiesce to his demands. Like every time she'd tried before, she couldn't make her jaw move. She couldn't set her lips to form the word. She couldn't get the air out to agree to his demands.

She just couldn't.

Or maybe she simply wouldn't.

She could say the word yes. Just not to the desire he stirred within her.

There was a part of Rose the gloried in the fact that he wanted this one thing from her. What would happen if she gave it to him? Would he lose his desire for her?

She couldn't risk it. Not when she needed him so badly. If he knew, he would use it against her, and she was already at his mercy.

Her thighs were splayed wide. Her arms bound between them.

Ilia lifted her arms, using the fabric of her ruined shirt. He looped the twisted cotton over a notch on the headboard. Spreading her like an eagle.

Now, even if she wanted to say yes to his demands or no, she had no choice. What happened next wasn't her fault. It wasn't her choice. It was all Ilia.

Rose settled into her captivity as her blood pooled between her legs. Her heartbeat was loud in her ears. Her fingers tingled from their constraints, as did her toes. She felt like she was flying.

Belatedly, she wondered if Ilia might take her flying in his dragon form.

Flying had to be the last thing on Ilia's mind. The fat head of his penis brushed against her sex. As he claimed her mouth with drugging kisses, that slick head licked at her opening. It didn't delve inside like his tongue did. Not even when she squirmed to get it closer.

It didn't matter how much she squirmed. She was being held down. She couldn't escape if she wanted. He could do anything he desired to her, and there was nothing she could do about it.

Rose lifted her hips, trying to give him a hint. Ilia ignored her. He rested on his side as he gazed down at her.

"You have the prettiest tits on the earth, sweet Rose. They look just like rosebuds." He pinched the rosebuds with his index and thumb, making the pink buds turn red. "They're nice little handfuls. Get used to me grabbing them every day."

Rose's body had been grabbed at and manhandled since her curves had developed. She used to glory in the days when she could lie alone in her bed with no one touching or even looking at her. Now, she couldn't imagine a day without Ilia's rough hands on her soft flesh.

"Don't shave this pretty pussy anymore. I want to bury my face in your nice, thick bush."

In answer, she could only whimper. All this dirty talk was doing nothing but increasing that heavy ache inside of her. It was making her hot with need for him.

Which was a biological reaction to him. Not a conscious decision on her part. Except she had never felt this wanton in her life.

She wanted Ilia.

She wanted his mouth.

She wanted his tongue.

She wanted his fingers.

And lord all mighty, she wanted his cock.

The desire for that long, thick hunk of flesh nestled between his thighs made her grow hot in her belly. Hotter than the first time when he'd bitten her. Only this time, it wasn't air that was filling her like a balloon. Now it felt like some molten material was coursing through her veins.

The hot lava surged up from her gut. It splashed into the tubes of her belly. Up and up, it swelled until it lodged in her throat. It forced her teeth to unclench, her lips to part. It took on air and was given voice.

"Yes," she said.

She thought it was a shout but realized it was only a whisper. Had he heard it?

Ilia went still for a long moment. His head cocked to the side like a predator who sensed prey nearby. His index and thumb loosened on her breast. He rolled his large body from its prone position on his side to hover over her.

This whole time, Rose had been trapped. In this second, she knew she could not escape. Not even if she wanted to try. In that moment of close scrutiny, Rose felt the urge to bolt.

She'd just made a fatal mistake. With that single *yes*, she had revealed her deepest desires. Ilia was looking at her differently. Like she was a wanton woman, a promiscuous slut who deserved the sneers that would come because she'd let him have her.

A second later, she lost all thought as Ilia thrust inside of her. One moment she was empty and worried. The next, she was full and sated. Rose let out a guttural yell as Ilia's dick filled her beyond her body's capacity.

It had been a long time since she'd lost her virginity. She'd only done it the once. Her body was not prepared for the assault.

Didn't matter. Her inner walls rearranged themselves to take Ilia in. Her muscles clamped hard to keep him there.

Rose tugged at her binds, needing to get free, to touch him in return. But she couldn't. She wanted to spread her thighs wider. But she was bound from doing so. She wanted to arch her hips higher. But the ties that held her prevented her from it.

Ilia pumped into her. Hard. Fast. And oh, so deep.

Was this sex he was doing to her? It couldn't be the same thing. It had felt nothing like this before.

The first and only time, there had been irritation and pain. This was more pleasure and bliss than Rose thought was possible.

She was so full that she couldn't take in any air—and she needed more air. She needed to beg Ilia to do it again, to give her even more. All she could get to come out of her throat were mewls and moans.

Luckily, Ilia didn't need any words. He never stopped his motions. Withdrawing and thrusting inside her again and again. His body moved impossibly faster. The sensations of fullness, of completeness, of wholeness sent Rose's brain into overdrive.

Yes came along with each inhale. *Please* came out with every exhale.

Before she knew it, that delicious pressure was building within her. The ascent was as quick as the descent. Waves of pleasure crashed over Rose as Ilia continued to thrust inside her. Her body shook from the impact. The impact went on and on as he held her tight, still pumping in and out of her as though both their lives depended on the motion.

Ilia's hand was between them. He rubbed at the oversensitive nub at the apex of her sex. As though he were performing a magic trick, the nub grew for him. It swelled with the hot pressure that had been gathering from somewhere deep inside.

He didn't stop his thrusting as he touched her, not for one second. His fingers worked their magic as his cock made itself at home inside her. A new climax was building in Rose, this one deeper than the last. When it crashed around her, Ilia still had a hold of her.

His hands were in her hair, tugging her head back, exposing her neck. She felt his teeth sink into that warm spot where he'd marked her before. She felt that pinprick of incisors at her neck, the biting warmth of his bite. When he pulled at her flesh, she felt herself clenching around him again.

"Come for me, sweet Rose."

Her body shook and jerked. She no longer had control of herself. She had to do what he commanded of her. She had no choice. Because he was right, she was his.

Ilia pulled her impossibly closer. He threw his head back and roared. His eyes went dragon bright.

Rose saw the beast within him staring back at her. In its gaze, it asked her the same question the man had asked her before. But the beast didn't ask. It demanded.

"Mine," it growled low and deep.

"Yes," she whispered, unable to deny it any longer.

CHAPTER NINETEEN

Ilia felt restless and at peace at the same time. His body hummed with satisfaction, but he wanted more of Rosc.

He'd never enjoyed the aftermath of sex when fairies wanted to cuddle him. He'd always found their bodies too sweet to rest beside. Their limbs too wiry and smooth.

Rose had flesh to her bones. There were curves that he could cling to. There was salt on her skin that he found intoxicating.

He wanted her again. He wanted her always. But he could stay content just as they were.

She'd said yes. True, it had been in the throes of passion. But that might be the only admission he'd ever get from Rose.

She was a complicated woman with her inability to ask for what she needed sexually. Though Ilia realized she didn't hesitate when it came to her sister. He knew that kind of love and devotion from his own brothers.

Even though they didn't always respect his dibs, Ilia knew they would never leave him out in the cold as their father had done. Over the years of his life, he'd seen time and again that as he fought for every scrap, and ounce, and inch that came his way, his brothers were often the ones tossing him food, making way for him, and giving him a hand.

He likely owed them a thank you. But he doubted it truly needed to be said. It had taken the dragons a lot of time and heartache to become the family they were today. Now, Ilia would make a family of his own with his mate.

He looked forward to a lifetime with Rose. She would keep him on his toes and keep his dick hard. It was hard now as he watched her slumber in his arms.

Ilia had fucked his mate into a coma. He'd lost track of how many times her tight sheath had squeezed around his cock. The last time it had, she'd let out a sigh of utter contentment and closed her eyes. She hadn't opened them again.

With great care, Ilia untied her feet from the bedpost. He took a few moments to massage each of her feet to ensure the circulation was still working there. As he caressed each of her toes in turn, he wondered if he might be developing a foot fetish. He had the urge to place each toe into his mouth.

The same desires happened when it came time to free her arms from the sleeves of her wrecked shirt. With his thumbs, he rubbed at the skin on the underside of her forearm. He traced the veins that pumped her life's blood, a little concerned that she was so thin that he could make out some of her bones.

He would fix that. He would ply her with food. Not that he was the best cook in the castle. But he would hunt the largest game for her, just like Arnold did in *Predator.* He wondered if she'd like mastodon?

Rose stirred in his arms. With her eyes still closed, her feet scissored together. As her thighs pressed together, she let out a pleasurable sounding moan. Ilia could guess why. He could see that her slick folds were still nice and plump and red from all of his attentions.

Her hand traveled down there. When her fingers found her swollen flesh, she gasped, her eyes flashing open. When her gaze met his, her cheeks reddened.

"Go on," he said. "You have my permission to touch yourself."

The embarrassment leached from her high cheeks to be replaced with ire. "It's my body. I don't need your permission."

Ilia rolled on top of her, trapping both their fingers in the crook of her tender folds. "You're wrong, sweet Rose. This is my pussy. You gave it to me last night."

"No, I didn't."

"Yes," he plunged two fingers into her, "you did."

She stopped arguing. Instead, she ground her hips against his fingers and let out a low moan.

"Do you want me to stop? You know what to say if you do."

"Stop. Please."

She turned her face, but Ilia caught her grin. He also caught onto the fact that she didn't use her safe word.

"No, Ilia. I can't take anymore." The words were muffled as she writhed against his fingers.

"You're going to come for me, sweet Rose. And then you're going to say thank you."

She opened her mouth. What came out was a low

guttural moan as her swollen folds shivered and clenched around his fingers. At the end of her sigh, her lips split into a wide grin as she said, "Fuck you."

Ilia chuckled as he put her fingers into his mouth and sucked.

Rose watched him. There was a light in her bright eyes. They were brighter than they were yesterday. It was as though someone had flipped the switch on inside her. But then they dimmed.

"Why did you leave?" she said. "After you marked me."

Ilia licked the last of her essence from his index finger. With the taste of her now gone from his fingers, he dipped his head, his chin settling on his chest in guilt. "Because I wanted to throw you down and fuck you."

"You did throw me down and fuck me."

"Yes, but that was after I knew you wanted it. Before that, I thought I was going to break my word to you. I had to get away. It was my fairy friend Marigold who made me realize your no's might mean yes."

"Marigold?" All the bright light faded from Rose's gaze now. Storm clouds, thunder, and lightning threatened.

"She's just a friend. Why? Are you jealous?"

"No," Rose huffed, crossing her arms over her breasts and turning away from him.

The scent of her jealousy was spicier than her arousal. "She's not the one to worry about. Two other fairies offered to console me."

Rose's hands balled into fists. She let out an indignant puff of air. Her legs kicked, trying to get the sheet he'd thrown over her off. Ilia threw an arm over her and locked her in place.

"I told them no," he said. "They didn't listen at first. Wouldn't take no for an answer. That's when I realized you might not mean what you say you mean."

Rose let out another huff of air. But she wasn't trying to get away from him anymore. Not that Ilia would've let her go if she'd truly tried.

"That's when I realized you might want me, even if you couldn't say the words."

Rose opened her mouth as though to deny it. Then shut her mouth when the denial didn't come.

"It's all right, sweet Rose. You don't have to admit it." He kissed her mouth, slow and languorous. "Not with these lips…"

Between her legs, Ilia's fingers sought her warm heat again. Rose reached down as though to shove him away. But then her fingers mixed with his, and their combined digits stroked her sex.

"With these lips," he said as she gasped her pleasure.

Ilia loved the sound. He loved all her sounds. Her pants of desire. Her biting taunts of frustration. All of it.

After they brought her to pleasure with their hands, he wrapped both their hands around his dick and they stroked him into ecstasy. They lay there sated, basking in the aftermath of their shared pleasure.

"Yes."

It was the tiniest whisper from Rose's lips. The word had been brewing in her chest for a while now. Ever since Ilia had looked at her with those bright, devil may care eyes and grinned at her as though he'd eat her up.

She'd wanted to shout yes then. But as always, the word stayed locked in a cage inside her chest.

Except now… now it wanted out.

"Yes," she said again. The word coming out on a stronger, more forceful gust of air from her lungs.

Rose was pretty pleased with the volume that time. Too bad Ilia wasn't awake to hear it.

She settled down into the cradle of his massive chest. There were scars there. Long jagged lines that looked like they'd come from claws. They were thick keloids, which meant the raised bumps were old. Likely there since childhood. Had his father done this to him?

Rose couldn't imagine any beast, big or small, that could best her Ilia.

Her Ilia?

Yes. *Her* Ilia.

Yes, he was hers. Yes, she was his. "Yes."

Ilia's eyes flashed open. Rose tried to suck the air back into her mouth. It was too late. The sound was already out in the air between them. She shifted to get off the mattress. Ilia's hands struck out to grab her around the waist.

"We're you trying to run, sweet Rose?"

"No," she said. Rose took a deep breath as the denial swallowed down the agreement she'd wanted to gift him. Now it sat at the bottom of her belly.

Ilia only smiled. He rubbed his thumb back and forth over her navel as though he knew exactly where the affirmation had drifted.

"I was just going to go clean up," she said.

"You're perfect." He wrapped his hands around her hips and brought her sweet pussy to his face. "Let me clean you up."

"Ilia." She wriggled halfheartedly. She didn't try

to get away from him. She was exactly where she wanted to be. Soon, she'd be able to tell him exactly what she wanted.

Soon.

"Hold still, woman. I'm licking for buried treasure."

"Am I your captive?"

"You're mine," he said, bringing her hips to sit on his chest. "I'm your hero. I'm your villain. Hell, I'll be your sidekick. I'll be whatever you need."

Rose tried to swallow. But the desire kept flooding into her mouth. That yes was rising on it.

"Tell me what you need, sweet Rose."

It rose up from her belly. It swelled into her chest. It was on the tip of her tongue, ready to walk that plank and dive into what was between them.

Ilia watched her intently. Waiting with the patience of a saint who knew he'd earned his right to divinity. But, in a flash, his gaze brightened. The dragon peered out from behind his eyes. His lips curled into a snarl, and he let out a low, menacing growl.

"Ilia?"

Ilia tossed Rose down on the mattress. He climbed over her as he bolted to the window. For a moment, Rose could only gape at his dark form standing tall against the moonlight. But the menace that rolled off him made her shiver.

"Ilia? Ilia, what's wrong?"

"I smell fur." The muscles in his back rippled. Rose could see the impression of wings under his skin. His flesh shimmered to scales and back again. "They're here."

"Who? Who's here?"

"The others."

Ilia shoved himself into a pair of pants. He was out the door with a growl, "Stay here," before she could ask any questions.

"Yeah, right," she said as she pulled a robe over her naked form. She belted it with some rope she found in his closet. It worked as perfectly as a wrap dress.

Rose crept down the hall. At the top of the steps, she saw the other women gathered in a huddle. Rose made her way to Lily, who had a handful of what looked like candied flowers that she was slipping into her mouth one at a time.

Despite knowing that they were in some type of danger, Rose took a moment to marvel at the change in her and Lily's circumstances. They never had to go on another predatory casting call or walk a slippery catwalk while balancing on a six-inch spike, or strip down to their unmentionables in freezing cold weather. Not only could they keep their bellies full, there was the opportunity to have their hearts fill up as well.

Elek had said that he and Rhoyl weren't interested in mating. But maybe there would be another dragon shifter around who might catch Lily's eye. Or maybe Lily didn't want to date. Maybe she was happy being on her own in a family that would take care of her and not use her.

"We know you're harboring two human females inside this castle," said a woman's voice.

Or at least Rose assumed it was a woman. There was nothing high-pitched about the voice. It was more rumbling growl than anything. Looking down the stairs, Rose saw the owner of the voice. She was a muscled woman with thick forearms. Her golden-bronze hair radiated from the crown of her head making her look like a lioness.

She was surrounded by a couple of other golden-haired males. There was also a dark-haired man with silver stripes in his hair. And another man that was even taller and thicker than Ilia.

Speaking of Ilia, Corun and Beryl both had a hand on him. No, strike that. They both had two hands on him, as though they were holding him back from attacking.

"I'm happy to settle this the old way," said the lioness woman, her gaze on Ilia.

"No, Leona," said Kimber. "We will not resort to the ways of our fathers. We will not fight."

"I'm not going to fight," Ilia snarled. Despite his words, his brothers didn't let loose their hold on him. "There's no need when I've already claimed what's mine."

Leona flashed her eyes at him like a cat. Like a very large cat. "We all agreed-"

Kimber cut her off. "We all agreed that the next women to cross over into the Veil would choose of her own free will."

"And yet we find two healthy women locked away in your castle," said the tall, salt and pepper-haired man.

His posture wasn't one of aggression. Neither was the big bear of a man beside him. Only the woman, Leona, looked ready to fight.

They chose to be here," said Kimber.

"That wasn't the agreement," said Leona. "Every shifter gets a chance at her."

Leona's gaze shifted from the dragons surrounding the stairs and climbed the steps. Those bright cat eyes flashed at Rose and Lily. That's when it clicked in Rose's head.

Two women from beyond the Veil. Claiming. Every shifter gets a chance at her. A chance at them. At her and Lily.

"It doesn't matter to me if the merchandise is spoiled," said Leona, her gaze still on Rose and Lily. "Go on girls, give us a twirl. Show mama what you're working with."

Rose gulped as though she tasted something foul. She moved to Lily, who looked equally as ill. They were going to be put on display. All for these men or shifters or whatever they were to take their pick.

"She's mine," growled Ilia, as his brothers tightened their hold. "I marked her. I claimed her."

To another woman, that declaration of a relationship out in public might be considered sweet, romantic even. To Rose, it reeked of betrayal. It was the second time a man had boasted of her private affairs with him. Only this time, it hurt way worse because Ilia mattered to her.

"Fine," growled Leona. "But the other one is fair game."

All male gazes shifted off Rose to Lily. The candied flowers fell from her sister's hands. Lily's eyes glazed over in that look she always got on casting calls.

That looked that said she was nothing but a blank canvas. That look that said she'd allow others to paint on the mask of who she was. Because who she was didn't matter.

"Lil?"

But Lily couldn't hear her. Lily couldn't see her. She'd already retreated inside herself.

Ilia was standing before her, but Rose ignored him. There was nothing he could do. She peered over him until she found his brother.

"Elek? Help us? Please, mark her or claim her or whatever."

Elek took in a deep breath. He let it out on a long, low sigh. "I'm sorry. I cannot."

Rose's eyes stung as though his words had slapped her. But she couldn't cry yet. There was still a chance. When Rose looked to the topaz blue dragon, Rhoyl wouldn't meet her gaze.

So much for family sticking together. The only person she could ever count on was her own blood. And right now, Lily needed Rose to be her hero.

Rose knew what she had to do. She inhaled a full breath, pushing down the yes that had bubbled so close to the surface only moments ago. She opened her eyes and did what she had to do.

"You want to be my hero?" she said to Ilia.

"I am your hero," he said.

"Then claim my sister."

"I can't do that. I've already claimed you."

"Take it back. Take it back and claim her. She needs your protection. I need you to protect her."

Ilia looked from Lily, who remained catatonic, and back to Rose. His once-over of Lily held only a spark of emotion. His gaze upon Rose was a blaze.

"Rose…" He reached for her.

She snatched her hand away. "No."

Ilia reached for her again.

"No," she said. "Vernon."

The color drained from Ilia's face. Like a light going out, his eyes went dull and dim. His strong hands, which had given her so much pleasure and certainty, went limp at his sides.

Rose took the opportunity to shove her sister at Ilia. He caught Lily like a ball he would take no joy in playing with. But he received it because it was his duty as Player One.

"Some claiming," said Leona. "She doesn't even remember the whelp's name."

CHAPTER TWENTY-ONE

It had taken two of his brothers to hold him back when the shifters entered the castle. As Rose walked out the front door and into the new day's sun, Ilia could barely hold himself up.

She'd told him no—a real no. She'd left him. She didn't want him. And why would she?

Some hero he was. He wasn't a hero at all. Once again, he'd been tossed out of the game. Put on the sidelines. At least this time, he was inside the house and not fighting for scraps like when his father had discarded him as worthless.

Ilia had fought tooth and claw to prove the male wrong. And he had. He'd survived then. Only now…? How was he to survive when his heart had stopped?

He couldn't fight right now if he'd tried. That single word—the word he'd given Rose to prove she was safe with him—she'd hurled it into his face. It had been a barrel thrown at Jump Man's head by Donkey Kong. It had been a turtle shell that clipped his feet out from under him, like in Super Mario Brothers. Ilia sat on the ground, powered down as his mate walked out the door.

If she had walked out with Leona and the lions, or the wolves, or the bears, Ilia's beast would've torn off his skin and slaughtered each one of them, breaking the Accords his brothers had fought so hard to make. That would have destroyed the fragile peace in the Veil.

Rose didn't leave with a shifter. She left with Cardi, Poppy, and Beryl. They would take her to God's Teet, to the apartment where Cardi stayed for a short time during her bout of independence. There Rose would stay until it was the time of the choosing. She'd made it clear she wouldn't choose him. She demanded he choose her sister.

"Rose?"

Ilia turned to glance at Lily. She was finally coming out of her catatonic state. She looked lost and fragile, like a little girl. Nothing like the spirited woman that Ilia had fallen in love with. How had he ever thought to choose Lily over Rose?

"Rose?" Lily began to shiver. It didn't look like her trembling form would hold her weight.

Ilia stood and wrapped an arm around her. She was less than skin and bones. Rose was right; Lily was far too frail to be claimed by any other shifter.

"Where's Rose?"

Ilia looked into pale blue eyes, so much like Rose's. But not quite as bright. Lily was a true damsel. She needed a man to save her.

Ilia knew he was not that man.

He didn't want a damsel. He didn't want a woman who could barely stand on her own two feet. Ilia wanted a hero—no. Ilia wanted a heroine.

"Rose is going to be fine," she said as he pulled Lily into the protection of his arms, just as his heroine had commanded him to do.

Ilia squeezed her tight, trying to let Lily know that she was safe. Her sister had sent her the best protection this side of the Veil. Now Ilia would have to do what he must to protect them both.

"Ilia?" Kimber approached his younger brother with hands raised in surrender.

It was a pose dragons never took. They'd been taught at a young age to never show weakness.

"I'm fine," Ilia said to his brother as he rubbed soothing circles with his palm into Lily's back.

"Did they take her away?" asked Lily, her voice slowly gaining strength. "Did those men take Rose away?"

"No," said Ilia, looking down at her. Her eyes were beginning to brighten, nearing the strength of her sister's. "Rose left on her own. But we're going to get her back."

"She has to choose, Ilia," said Kimber, regret lacing his deep voice. "Those are the rules we all agreed to."

"She'll choose me," said Ilia, his gaze still on Lily. "She'll choose me once she knows her sister is safe."

"How are we going to do that?" asked Corun.

There was a part of Ilia that wanted to smirk. Corun fancied himself the smartest of the weyr. But here, Ilia, the runt, had figured out how to solve the problem.

"Simple," said Ilia.

He looked to Elek and Rhoyl, who stood off to the side. Neither met his eyes. Both of their gazes were cast down in shame.

"I've recently learned that no doesn't always mean no."

CHAPTER TWENTY-TWO

ose's stomach was in turmoil. Her gut twisted into knots that tightened and squeezed until she doubled over. Arms came around her. The arms weren't strong or muscular like Ilia's. These arms were the same size and skin tone as hers, but there was a strength to them. There was also chemical soapy spray above the arms, like a can of hairspray had bloomed.

"It's going to be okay," Cardi said as she tightened her hold around Rose.

Rose knew a lie when she heard one. She'd just said the mother of all lies to the man she'd fallen in love with. Not the part about Ilia protecting her sister. Rose absolutely meant that. She would die for Lily.

But that bit about Rose not needing Ilia to be her hero? Yeah, complete and utter bullshit. The proof was in her belly, which was roiling in protest as they went further and further away from the castle.

All around them, flowers lifted their blooming heads as they walked by, just like in Rose's dream. Trees bent their boughs to gaze down at them. Slender males and females of every shade of the rainbow stopped and stared quizzically.

Rose couldn't appreciate the wondrous views that would've had casting directors falling over themselves and photographers clicking. She was too far in her head, worrying over the dilemma she'd gotten herself in.

She'd be going on a casting call soon enough. One where she'd have lifetime employment depending on who chose her.

At the end of the path, they came to what looked like a neighborhood bar. Rose had never been inside a bar. There was no point. Back in her world, she couldn't hold a meal, much less her liquor. But one whiff of the sweet and spicy scent of alcohol, and she knew she wanted to be drunk.

"Hey, Mari," said Cardi. "Can I get three Apple Eves, please? Go hard on the snake venom, would you?"

The bartender, Mari, didn't move into action at Cardi's order. Her slender indigo arms crossed over her chest. Her sky blue gaze fixed on Rose. Rose felt a decided chill in the air.

"Is this her?" asked Mari. "Is this Ilia's new mate?"

Cardi opened her mouth to respond but then winced and pressed her lips together. Poppy leaned back into Beryl's embrace. Their dubious expressions matched each other.

The word no refused to pass Rose's lips. That same yes that had been rising up inside her for Ilia didn't want to present itself to this woman. It was for Ilia. Though now she wouldn't be able to give it to him.

"Are you Elek's then?" asked Mari. "Did that monk finally decide to play his V-card?"

There was a chorus of tinkling giggles from behind her. Rose glanced over her shoulder to see a few other women. Though to call them women didn't seem right. They looked like they were walking Photoshopped caricatures of models. They were absolute perfection. Not a single blemish on their pastel skin. Their bodies had achieved a thinness that New York and Paris runways would've killed for.

"You've been marked," Mari was saying. "I can see the bite from here. If you're not Ilia's or Elek's... you can't be Rhoyl's. He wouldn't..."

Rose turned back to the bar. Her hand went to the mark on her collarbone under Mari's ice gold glare. Mari backed away, her hand going to the exact same place on her neck, which was covered by her dull-looking sack.

"I'll get someone else to serve you. I'm taking my break." Mari turned on her heel, dashing into a back room of the bar.

Through the front door came another crash. The lion shifters from before strode into the bar. Their golden manes illuminated the room, but not as brightly as their sharp-toothed smirks lit up the room. They were followed by the thick bear of a man and the other one with the wolfish grin.

The lioness Leona wasn't with them, which is probably the reason why Rose relaxed. Despite the beasts that lived in them, they were just men. Men all wanted the same thing; sex.

She'd been prepared to have meaningless sex with Ilia. Except his touches came to mean the world to her. She couldn't imagine having another man's hands on her body. But pretty soon, one of them would claim the right to.

Her gut roiled some more, threatening to give up everything Rose had consumed the day before. She took a deep breath to hold it down. She had to do this. Lily would've never survived it. Ilia would take care of her sister. He'd keep her safe and care for her. That would have to sustain Rose for the rest of her life.

"Tell me about the others," Rose said, looking between Cardi on her right and Poppy on her left. "Who don't I want to be chosen for."

"You misunderstand," said Beryl. "They do not get to choose. You are the prize. You make the choice."

"They'll put themselves on display," Cardi said. "Showing off their best assets in hopes that you'll choose them."

Well, that was novel. Rose would be the casting director in this situation. Already she could see causes to reject the men.

That lion had a mane of hair that went down his back, reminding her of Fabio. Too 80s for her. The other sported a mohawk reminding her of a blond Mr. T, complete with a gold chain around his neck. Thank you, next.

The dark bear of a man was the size of Andre the Giant. He'd likely crush her with just his thumb. The man with the wolfish grin looked too confident. Like a used car salesman. Like he knew he had the job in the bag.

He was wrong. They were all wrong. She wanted to reject each of them and send them home. Because she'd already cast this role.

She'd chosen Ilia. How could she not choose Ilia? He was the true hero of her dreams. He was the villain to her doubts and nightmares.

She didn't need this job. She didn't want this job. If they were going to fight over her and her sister, then that was their problem. Not hers. She would fight back.

Rose pushed away from the bar. She only got two steps before the shifters were in front of her, crowding her space.

"Allow me to introduce myself," said the mohawk'd lion. "I'm—"

"I don't care," said Rose, sidestepping him.

There was a chorus of deep belly laughs. Then the guy with the wolfish grin was beside her.

"Not interested," Rose said as she stepped away from him as well.

A low growl sounded behind her, but it didn't deter her. She balled her fist the way Ilia had taught her. She'd strike out if she needed to.

But no one grabbed her as she went out the doors. The fresh air hit her square in the chest once she was outside. Her stomach settled, her mind cleared. She knew exactly what she had to do.

The only problem was, she didn't know which way to go. She'd need the girls and Beryl to lead her back to the castle, back to Ilia.

Rose turned to head back inside. She was only able to turn partway around to the door. A cloud of dark smoke plumed in her face. With one inhale, she lost control of her limbs. Arms came around her, and she was being lifted, carried… kidnapped. Again.

CHAPTER TWENTY-THREE

Ilia flew hard to reach God's Teet. He knew Rose was in no danger with Beryl on one side and Cardi on the other. Most in the Veil feared Cardi more than her mate Kimber. Ilia pushed his wings so hard because he couldn't stand to be another moment without his mate.

Rose had asked him to keep her sister safe. He'd done that. With his actions now, no shifter would dare sniff around Lily. But he knew they were all sniffing around his own mate.

With that thought, his wings picked up enough power to break the sound barrier. He landed at the door of Cardi's old apartment with a loud thud. The floorboards creaked under his weight as he shifted from beast to man.

He was naked, but he didn't care. He didn't need clothes for what he had planned for Rose. He was itching to get her back into bed and tie her up like a damsel. It would be pure role play because his Rose was the farthest thing from a helpless woman.

She was a true hero, coming to her sister's rescue. Only now, Ilia insisted on coming to her rescue. He would be her hero, her villain, her sidekick. Anything she wanted or needed. But he would be hers, and she would be his.

He smelled the shifters below. But he felt no need to fight. He'd already won, and now he would reclaim his prize.

Except the apartment was dark. Silent. Empty.

Rose wasn't there. But he could smell her scent. She was near. Maybe she was at the bar?

Ilia grabbed a pair of Kimber's pants. His brother and Cardi liked to escape to the apartment from time to time to be alone. With his lower half covered, he entered the bar.

The first thing he spotted were two redheads. There were Cardi's curls that were teased high to the ceiling. There was Poppy's soft whisps of hair that rested on her shoulders. Where were Rose's soft waves of red?

Ilia sniffed the air again. She was here. Somewhere. Having his mate in such close proximity while not in his arms was pushing his dragon too far.

"Beryl," Ilia growled loud enough to be heard over the music. "Where is she?"

His brother didn't need to ask who Ilia was talking about. "She's right…"

Beryl looked around. His features growing dimmer with each corner he looked in to find that Rose wasn't there.

"She was just standing next to me," said Cardi. "Maybe she went into the bathroom."

Cardi came out of the girl's restroom a moment later without Rose. Ilia's attention turned to the shifters in the room. He stormed up to Ari, giving the lion's long mane a nasty tug.

"Where's my mate?"

Ari turned a golden glare on Ilia. "Do I look like I have your mate?"

Ari held out his hands. He opened his massive palms, revealing nothing inside. Nothing except ink marks. Likely from writing his awful poetry.

Ilia turned to Ari's brother Kefir, who also didn't appear to be harboring a svelte redhead in his paws.

Neither were the wolf or bear red-handed. But she was nearby. He could smell her. Could she be hiding? That wasn't the character of the woman he knew. She wouldn't cower for any of these men.

"What do you care," said Kefir. "She denied your claim. Your supposed mate tossed you aside."

He was wrong. Rose hadn't tossed him aside. She'd trusted him with what she held most dear. Not one of these males understood that, which meant that not one of them was worthy to breathe her air.

But they were all sharing the same air. She was here. And she needed him. She needed him just as much as he needed her.

For most of his life, Ilia swore he never needed anyone. He swore he would be his own hero. He never cried out for help. Even though his brothers were always there at hand. Beryl stood at his side, along with Cardi and Poppy. He could ask for their help. Instead, Ilia threw his head back and cried out.

"Rose! Rose, where are you?"

The bar went silent under his bellow. There were whispers and a few giggles at his outburst. Ilia didn't care if he looked like a weakling calling out for his love. What he did care about was that Rose didn't so much as make a peep.

Was it possible that she was hiding? Was it possible she didn't want to be found by anyone, including him? Was it possible she didn't want him?

His heart rejected that notion. He knew what rejection felt like. Rose hadn't rejected him. She still needed him. She still wanted him. He knew that in his warm blood. He just needed to find her.

And then he heard it. It was so silent. Barely audible. But he heard her whisper his name.

"Ilia?"

His name was the first thing on her lips as Rose began to come back to awareness. She knew something was wrong when instead of the spicy scent of him, she smelled the cloying sweetness of flowers.

She couldn't move her arms or legs. They were bound tight. But not with soft cloth or biting rope. This substance felt sharp and at the same time sticky like she'd been tied up with blades of grass.

When Rose cracked an eye open, she saw that that was exactly what she was tied up in. Vines wrapped around her skin, twining her limbs like threaded cables. Grass was below her as well. Her entire body slid against the ground as she was dragged into the night.

Above Rose was a green-skinned woman with pointy ears. Vines extended from her fingers as she tugged Rose along. Beside her was a pastel blue woman whose hair looked like the pollen of a flower. The woman nodded her head in agreement at whatever the green one was saying. Tiny puffs of gold drifted down toward Rose, and she sneezed.

"You've got to be kidding me." Rose groaned after her sneezing fit was over. "I've been kidnapped by fairies?"

"Oh, this isn't a kidnapping, dear," said the green one with the vines shooting out of her hands. "If someone kidnaps you, they want to keep you. This is a return."

"A return?" asked Rose, though her voice was muffled as she was dragged through the grass. Luckily, the earth was soft and warm, so she got no bumps or bruises. That didn't mean she was enjoying the ride.

"We're taking you back to the Veil and tossing you onto the other side."

"Tossing me back? Why?"

"We're tired of you little warmbloods coming to

our world and stealing our beasts," said the blue, golden-haired one.

"Your beasts?" asked Rose.

"They're all fighting over you," hissed the golden fairy. Though the hiss came out like tinkling wind chimes. "Do you know how long it's been since I got laid?"

"She means properly laid," said the green one as though Rose had asked for clarification. "Male fairies are great lovers, but not one of them can bend your vines like a beast. Am I right?"

The women shared secret smiles under the pale moonlight. Rose could only glance between the two of them. Her heart began to pump as it sensed she was in real danger. If she went back to the other side of the Veil, she would be sick again. She would never see Lily again. And worse, she would never see Ilia again.

"No," Rose shouted. When the fairies paid her no heed, she shouted, "Vernon!"

Unfortunately, neither of the bloom-headed women knew what that meant. Only one person in the whole world knew what it meant. Come to think of it, Rose didn't exactly know the reference as she'd never seen *The Breakfast Club.* So she didn't know who the villain principal was. As soon as she got out of this and got back to Ilia, they would sit down and watch the film together.

With that thought, Rose felt a surge of energy. She had to get away from these batty blooms before they killed her by tossing her back. She balled her hand into a fist. Twisting and turning at the wrist, she managed to work one hand free. But she had the rest of her body to work free of the vines.

She couldn't think of that now. She set her mind to thinking of Ilia. But thoughts of him only made her heart ache. Especially the last sight of him when she had rejected him.

She had cast him aside, just like his father had done when he was a baby. Rose imagined that had been the same look Ilia must have worn as a child when the one person in the world who was supposed to love him threw him away like trash. She couldn't have that as the last thing he thought of her. She needed him to know that she loved him.

With that thought, Rose managed to get a whole arm free. Now that she had an arm loose, she was able to do a little damage. And she knew exactly what she wanted to maim.

Rose struck out with her fist, open-handed. Her nails struck the green fairy's ankle. The fairy let out an ear-piercing screech that made birds jump out of tree branches and fly high into the night.

The screech also made the fairy loosen her grip on the vines holding Rose. The vines coming out of her fingers snapped back under her nails, like a switchblade being closed. The fairy's green hand let go of Rose to grasp at her bruised ankle.

Suddenly Rose was free. Unfortunately, her freedom came at a cost. Without the green fairy holding onto Rose, Rose's still-bound form began to tumble away from the fairies.

Rose picked up momentum as she went tumbling down a hill. With only one arm free, she had no way to stop herself. The end of the hill was coming up quick. It was a dark ravine that—if she fell down into—she had no way of getting herself back out.

Rose opened her mouth and screamed the only thing that mattered, "Ilia, save me!"

CHAPTER TWENTY-FIVE

he sound of birds crying in the night air muted the sound Ilia had thought he'd heard. No, it wasn't a thought. It was a fact. He had heard Rose call out to him.

She was in danger. Every sense in his body told him so. His ears led him outside the bar. His hands told him she had just slipped through his grasp. His nose picked up her trail—though it was faint. There was a strong floral scent covering Rose's heady essence.

Ilia's gaze scanned the immediate area for movement. He saw none except the birds circling up in the sky. They moved as though they'd been disturbed from their perch.

Ilia moved in that direction. He took one step on

foot, his bare heel crunching the rocks into pebbles. By the second step, he was in the air. His wings unfolded from his back, and his dragon took over.

The beast's sense of smell and sight was far superior to the man's. Those senses would be needed to track Rose. But the beast needed the man's reasoning and deduction to stay on track.

What was she doing out here? Perhaps she was trying to find her way back to the castle. Back to him.

"Vernon!"

That was definitely Rose's voice. Her safe word wasn't whispered in desperation for him to understand this time. No, it was shouted. As though she was desperate for whatever was happening to her now to cease immediately.

Ilia didn't stop. Not for a single second. He pushed himself toward that sound.

His Rose was in danger. She needed a hero. She needed him.

Up ahead, he spotted Clove and Honeysuckle. That had been the floral scent he'd smelled atop Rose's. Clove was bent over, her green hands rubbing at sap oozing from her ankle. Honeysuckle was peering down into the darkness of a ravine. Rose was nowhere in sight.

Ilia dipped low to ask the two fairies if they'd seen his beloved when he heard a sharp cry.

"Ilia, save me!"

The sound came from the ravine. It took his mind two precious seconds to piece the scene together. That was Rose calling out to him for help. Her voice came from inside the deep belly because she had somehow toppled over the cliff and fallen into the ravine.

Ilia stopped thinking. He bolted into action. Zipping past Clove and Honeysuckle, he dove into the ravine. He had to pull his wings into his back to avoid the sides of the rocky cliff.

It was still a tight fit. The jagged rocks tore at his body. He ignored every ache and pain as he dove for Rose.

She was tumbling down the rock face. She'd reach the bottom within seconds. And then…

Ilia didn't waste a moment on that thought. It didn't matter because it wasn't going to happen. He was here to save the day, to save the woman he loved.

She was almost within his grasp. Just another inch or two. To reach, he'd need to retract his wings even more. To do that, he would freefall, and they would both crash to the bottom.

Ilia slapped his wings into his sides. That was enough space to give him purchase. He reached out his claw and… got her.

He brought Rose into his body, pulling her tightly against his chest. Once she was secure, he flung his wings out to wrap them around the both of them. The impact was brutal, but he took the brunt of it. When the pebbles settled and the ground was at his back, Ilia finally unwrapped his wings and shifted back into human form.

"You saved me," Rose breathed.

"Of course, I saved you." Ilia brushed pebbles from her hair. "It's what I was born to do."

There were tears in Rose's eyes as her mouth worked. Ilia waited patiently for the shock to wear off, and she could find her words. As he waited, he noticed for the first time that she was bound in vines. He didn't get a chance to ask her about it because words were spilling from her lips.

Actually, not words. Just one word.

"Yes," Rose said. "Yes," she repeated. The affirmation started as a whisper. With each repetition, it grew stronger and stronger until she was shouting it.

"Yes, what, sweet Rose?"

"Yes, everything. Yes, anything. Yes, you."

A lump formed in Ilia's throat. There were so many words he wanted to get out, so much he wanted to say to her. Every single word he tried stalled. Words, phrases, full sentences formed a backlog in his chest. Rose didn't appear to need to hear any of his words. She had more to say.

"They were going to take me back to the Veil and toss me over to the other side."

Something got past Ilia's backlog then. It was a growl.

It was Clove's vines that bound Rose now. Ilia would deliver Clove and Honeysuckle to the fairy king, Gyges, himself. That sadistic fae liked to come up with gruesome punishments that damaged the mind as well as the body. It was exactly the fate the two of them deserved.

"All I could think was that I would never see you again, and you would believe I didn't want you."

"I never believed that," Ilia said. "I knew better."

"I love you."

He grinned. "I knew that, too. But it is nice to hear. Say it again."

Her gaze narrowed on him, and she pursed her lips. Ilia's cock twitched at the thought he'd need to pleasure an agreement out of her. There would be no safe word that would save her from what he was planning to do to hear those three little words on repeat.

"Can you get me out of these vines, please? I don't want to be tied up by anyone or anything unless it's from you."

With the flick of a claw, Ilia freed Rose. The moment her limbs were free, she flung her arms around his neck. Then, for good measure, she wrapped her legs around his waist.

"I choose you," Rose said. "I love you. I'm going to fight for you. For you and Lily. You're both my family, and no one's taking either of you away from me."

"Lily's taken care of."

Rose pulled back to peer up at him. "She is?"

"You asked me to complete that task, and I did so. My brother agreed to mate her."

"Did I ever tell you you're my hero?"

Ilia took a deep breath, breathing those words in as he kissed his damsel in delight. He'd finally done it. He'd saved the day. He didn't have a princess in his arms. He held a heroine, the strongest player in any game.

Peace settled over him with the knowledge that he'd mastered this level. He had no interest in playing any more games. Not when he'd won in life.

EPILOGUE

The smell of alcohol burned Elek's nostrils. He put spirits in many of the foods he prepared for his family. However, he'd never once drunk any of the liquid straight from the bottle before.

This liquid had come straight from an old, dusty bottle at the top of the shelf of the bar. Mari hadn't bothered to remove any of the dust particles when she'd popped the cork and poured. Elek saw a few unsanitary bits floating around on the surface. Shouldn't any object sink once it was submerged in alcohol?

"Bottoms up," said Mari.

With one hand, the fairy shoved the mug into Elek's clenched fists. With her other hand, she downed a mug of her own, tipping the cup until all Elek could see was the bottom.

Elek wasn't a competitive dragon by nature. But when he saw the relief cross Mari's features after she downed the alcohol, he wanted that too. He brought the mug to his lips and tipped it back. Only to splutter, cough, and choke the moment the fiery liquid hit the back of his throat.

"Easy there, big guy. It's your first time."

This was Elek's first drink at God's Teet. He'd had a chaste fruit drink whenever he'd come in. Fairies would approach him, but he'd always wave them away, not interested in sullying himself with their flowery scents. He couldn't. The beast within him would easily break their flexible limbs if it got its claws on them.

"Just take it slow your first time," Mari was saying as she poured another drink for herself.

This certainly was a day of firsts for Elek. Other than Mari, no one had offered him the option to go slow. No one had even offered him to option to say no. Which Elek had said. Numerous times. But his wishes didn't rank high on this particular matter.

Elek raised the mug to his mouth again. He heeded Mari's warning of going slow this time when he drank. The liquid was smoother as it went down his throat this time, though it still burned.

Inside his gut, Elek felt the dragon stir. He used meditation techniques and kept himself away from all things excitable to keep his volatile dragon under the staunchest of control. He had to. He couldn't have a repeat of his shameful past.

"Here's to shedding past mistakes," said Mari.

Elek lifted his head, but then had to immediately close his eyes. The vision of Mari standing behind the bar multiplied into two, then back to one, then to three. Just two swallows of alcohol and he was already losing control, just like he'd done in his past. Though both he and his beast knew that alcohol hadn't been to blame back then.

"You can't shed your mistakes," he said. "They stay with you. All you can do is accept what you've done and try to make amends."

"I didn't do anything wrong," said Mari, her words slurring as she poured her third cup of drink. "I'm not the one that's gone and mated with a human after marking me."

"Marked you? I never marked you. I haven't even marked Lily yet. That's what the liquid courage is for." Elek raised the mug, and the liquid inside sloshed over the rim.

Mari's eyes went wide as snowballs. She let out a long sigh that was tinged with a cold front. "You claimed the human? Not…"

"Lily is mine. Not his."

The relief in Mari's icy features was instant. As though the sun had come up over the winter fairy's head. But her secret childhood love with Rhoyl was another story. Elek had his own drama to deal with.

No, Elek hadn't claimed Lily yet. He hadn't even marked her. He didn't trust himself to let out only his fangs. What if it happened again? What if the animal trapped inside of him nearly killed another woman?

Elek knew this had to be done. The other shifters would fight to claim Lily if she was unmated. Lily was far too fragile for that.

Elek had seen enough evidence of her fragility during the handful of days he'd known her. Lily was quiet, timid. She would retreat into herself if too many people were around. Much like Elek was prone to do when it got crowded.

Lily loved to eat. Elek was happy to feed her. He thrilled to watch her eat his food. She closed her eyes in ecstasy with each bite he prepared for her. Something below his belly button tightened at the memory of that.

It was the beast stirring in its cage. Elek took a deep cleansing breath, focusing on calm and peace and nothingness until the dragon's roars were doused. But he knew it was only a temporary fix. To save Lily, he'd have to let the beast out.

Both Elek and Lily will have to confront their past demons if they have any hope of claiming the love their wounded souls deserve.

Get ready for this heartfelt, steamy romance with a bite in
The Dragon's Compliant Sacrifice
the fifth book in the Last Dragons Series.

Want to know how the Veil became closed in the first place?
Read the forbidden romance that started it all when a Valkyrie fell for a dragon and a human sacrifice slipped back through the Veil while they were kissing.

The Valkyrie's Claim
is a free story written for my Reader Group.
If you'd like your copy, just come on over and
join us.
http://bit.ly/InesReaders

Lover of fairytales, folklore, and mythology, Ines Johnson spends her days reimagining the stories of old in a modern world. She writes books where damsels cause the distress, princesses wield swords, and moms save the world.

You can sign up for her mailing list and receive alerts and free reads at https://ineswrites.com/ReaderGroup.

The Last Dragons

The Dragon's Reluctant Sacrifice

The Dragon's Ambivalent Sacrifice

The Dragon's Willing Sacrifice

The Dragon's Rebellious Sacrifice

The Dragon's Compliant Sacrifice

The Dragon's Forbidden Sacrifice